Secrets of the Heart

At dinner, the Earl looked at Zenobia for a long moment before he said:

"Perhaps that is what you should be doing—sitting for an artist."

For a moment Zenobia did not realise that the Earl was paying her a compliment.

Then she saw an expression in his eyes that made her draw in her breath.

"You are very beautiful, Zenobia," the Earl said.

For a moment Zenobia was almost hypnotised by the deep tone of his voice. As he spoke he reached out and put his hand over hers.

With the swiftness of a frightened fawn, she pulled her hand from beneath the Earl's.

She rose to her feet.

"I think, My Lord," she said, "it is now . . . correct for me to . . . leave you to drink your . . . port."

Without looking at the Earl again she ran from the room, closing the door sharply behind her . . .

A Camfield Novel of Love
by Barbara Cartland

"Barbara Cartland's novels are all distinguished by their intelligence, good sense, and good nature . . ."

—ROMANTIC TIMES

"Who could give better advice on how to keep your romance going strong than the world's most famous romance novelist, Barbara Cartland?"

—THE STAR

Camfield Place,
Hatfield
Hertfordshire,
England

Dearest Reader,

Camfield Novels of Love mark a very exciting era of my books with Jove. They have already published nearly two hundred of my titles since they became my first publisher in America, and now all my original paperback romances in the future will be published exclusively by them.

As you already know, Camfield Place in Hertfordshire is my home, which originally existed in 1275, but was rebuilt in 1867 by the grandfather of Beatrix Potter.

It was here in this lovely house, with the best view in the county, that she wrote *The Tale of Peter Rabbit*. Mr. McGregor's garden is exactly as she described it. The door in the wall that the fat little rabbit could not squeeze underneath and the goldfish pool where the white cat sat twitching its tail are still there.

I had Camfield Place blessed when I came here in 1950 and was so happy with my husband until he died, and now with my children and grandchildren, that I know the atmosphere is filled with love and we have all been very lucky.

It is easy here to write of love and I know you will enjoy the Camfield Novels of Love. Their plots are definitely exciting and the covers very romantic. They come to you, like all my books, with love.

Bless you,

CAMFIELD NOVELS OF LOVE
by Barbara Cartland

THE POOR GOVERNESS
WINGED VICTORY
LUCKY IN LOVE
LOVE AND THE MARQUIS
A MIRACLE IN MUSIC
LIGHT OF THE GODS
BRIDE TO A BRIGAND
LOVE COMES WEST
A WITCH'S SPELL
SECRETS
THE STORMS OF LOVE
MOONLIGHT ON THE
  SPHINX
WHITE LILAC
REVENGE OF THE HEART
THE ISLAND OF LOVE
THERESA AND A TIGER
LOVE IS HEAVEN
MIRACLE FOR A MADONNA
A VERY UNUSUAL WIFE

THE PERIL AND THE
  PRINCE
ALONE AND AFRAID
TEMPTATION OF A
  TEACHER
ROYAL PUNISHMENT
THE DEVILISH DECEPTION
PARADISE FOUND
LOVE IS A GAMBLE
A VICTORY FOR LOVE
LOOK WITH LOVE
NEVER FORGET LOVE
HELGA IN HIDING
SAFE AT LAST
HAUNTED
CROWNED WITH LOVE
ESCAPE
THE DEVIL DEFEATED
THE SECRET OF THE
  MOSQUE

A DREAM IN SPAIN
THE LOVE TRAP
LISTEN TO LOVE
THE GOLDEN CAGE
LOVE CASTS OUT FEAR
A WORLD OF LOVE
DANCING ON A RAINBOW
LOVE JOINS THE CLANS
AN ANGEL RUNS AWAY
FORCED TO MARRY
BEWILDERED IN BERLIN
WANTED—A WEDDING RING
THE EARL ESCAPES
STARLIGHT OVER TUNIS
THE LOVE PUZZLE
LOVE AND KISSES
SAPPHIRES IN SIAM
A CARETAKER OF LOVE
SECRETS OF THE HEART

Other books by Barbara Cartland

THE ADVENTURER
AGAIN THIS RAPTURE
BARBARA CARTLAND'S
  BOOK OF BEAUTY AND
  HEALTH
BLUE HEATHER
BROKEN BARRIERS
THE CAPTIVE HEART
THE COIN OF LOVE
THE COMPLACENT WIFE
COUNT THE STARS
DESIRE OF THE HEART
DESPERATE DEFIANCE
THE DREAM WITHIN
ELIZABETHAN LOVER
THE ENCHANTING EVIL
ESCAPE FROM PASSION
FOR ALL ETERNITY
A GOLDEN GONDOLA
A HAZARD OF HEARTS
A HEART IS BROKEN
THE HIDDEN HEART
THE HORIZONS OF LOVE
IN THE ARMS OF LOVE

THE IRRESISTIBLE BUCK
THE KISS OF PARIS
THE KISS OF THE DEVIL
A KISS OF SILK
THE KNAVE OF HEARTS
THE LEAPING FLAME
A LIGHT TO THE HEART
LIGHTS OF LOVE
THE LITTLE PRETENDER
LOST ENCHANTMENT
LOVE AT FORTY
LOVE FORBIDDEN
LOVE IN HIDING
LOVE IS THE ENEMY
LOVE ME FOREVER
LOVE TO THE RESCUE
LOVE UNDER FIRE
THE MAGIC OF HONEY
METTERNICH THE
  PASSIONATE DIPLOMAT
MONEY, MAGIC AND
  MARRIAGE
NO HEART IS FREE
THE ODIOUS DUKE

OPEN WINGS
A RAINBOW TO HEAVEN
THE RELUCTANT BRIDE
THE SCANDALOUS LIFE
  OF KING CAROL
THE SECRET FEAR
THE SMUGGLED
  HEART
A SONG OF LOVE
STARS IN MY HEART
STOLEN HALO
SWEET ENCHANTRESS
SWEET PUNISHMENT
THEFT OF A HEART
THE THIEF OF LOVE
THIS TIME IT'S LOVE
TOUCH A STAR
TOWARDS THE STARS
THE UNKNOWN HEART
WE DANCED ALL NIGHT
THE WINGS OF ECSTASY
THE WINGS OF LOVE
WINGS ON MY HEART
WOMAN, THE ENIGMA

A NEW CAMFIELD NOVEL OF LOVE BY

BARBARA CARTLAND

Secrets of the Heart

JOVE BOOKS, NEW YORK

SECRETS OF THE HEART

A Jove Book / published by arrangement with
the author

PRINTING HISTORY
Jove edition / March 1988

ISBN: 0-515-09486-2

Jove Books are published by the Berkley Publishing Group,
200 Madison Avenue, New York, New York 10016.
The name "JOVE" and the "J" logo
are trademarks belonging to Jove Publications, Inc.

PRINTED IN THE UNITED STATES OF AMERICA

10 9 8 7 6 5 4 3 2 1

Author's Note

Her Majesty Queen Victoria opened the Colonial and India Exhibition at the Albert Hall on 1 May 1866. It was a great success and the Indian exhibits were astounding.

The Queen did her best to sustain the image of an expanding Empire, and the Foreign Secretary, Lord Rosebery, who was very romantic, begged her to bestow on this Imperial Occasion all the pomp possible.

"With all the pomp you like," the Queen replied, "as long as I do not have to wear a low dress."

She would also not break her rule of widowhood and wear her crown out of doors.

The enthusiasm for the Empire was justified—it extended over an area of approximately 11 million square miles and its population was 372 million.

chapter one

1885

THE train drew nearer to London.

Zenobia felt herself becoming more and more nervous.

She told herself it was ridiculous.

She had not been nervous when she and her father had climbed high mountains or drifted down a crocodile-infested river in a leaking Dhow.

Nor she remembered, when they lost their way in the desert under a burning sun.

But she was definitely frightened of meeting her Step-mother.

It would be very uncomfortable, to say the least of it.

Lord Chadwell had realised that his second wife, after three years of marriage, was being unfaithful to him.

He had not remonstrated with her or caused a scene.

Instead, he had simply walked out of the house.

He had taken his daughter, Zenobia, who closely re-sembled his first wife, with him.

He had then started, as he had always wanted to do, to explore the world.

Zenobia was the name he have given his daughter because he had always wanted to visit Palmyra.

Together they read all they could find about the famous Queen Zenobia of Palmyra.

The authors of *Augustan History* had described her as a "second Cleopatra."

When they left London Zenobia was only nine, but she soon learnt to be a companion her father loved, and she understood his thirst for knowledge.

This not only demanded seeing whatever country they were in, but really getting to know its people.

India was the first country they visited and they lived there for three years.

Zenobia found herself consorting with Princes and Maharajahs, fakirs and shop-keepers.

She enjoyed the company of men of every caste.

They had moved on to Ceylon and lived for a short time in Siam before they visited Cambodia and Bali.

Then, after being extremely uncomfortable in Burma, they had returned to India.

Not only Lord Chadwell but also Zenobia found its beauty and its people irresistible.

They did not return to England until Lord Chadwell felt he must commit to paper his experiences.

He hoped they would help and inspire other people, just as he had been by the countries in which he had lived.

But he made no attempt to contact his wife.

He had had no communication with her since he left.

Instead, he had bought a house in Devonshire near the sea.

He settled down, with his daughter's help, to write what he said was to be the book of his life.

"I want, my dearest," he said, "to describe how I have developed my instinct, my perception, and, most of all, my sensibilities, for that, I believe, is what all men and women should do, unless they are to waste the inexpressible value of being alive."

Zenobia thought, as he did, that the only way mankind could reach towards the infinite was to develop and train its powers of perception.

She knew exactly what her father was saying.

How, even as he had found the path of development, he wanted to share it with others.

Because they were always travelling, she had an unconventional education.

Her father was a very clever man, and she had learnt so much from him.

She therefore thought that extra tuition, when it came, was quite unnecessary.

But he was anxious that she should have professional teachers.

When she looked back, she thought they were certainly a strange assortment.

There were priests of various religions to teach her their scriptures.

Of these she found the Abbots of the Buddhist Monasteries far more interesting than any of the others.

There had been men and women of every nationality to instruct her in languages.

She was now fluent in all those which her father thought important, and she had picked up Urdu from their Indian servants.

She had learnt arithmetic simply by reason of her father leaving her to pay all the bills they accumulated.

She had to make sure they had enough money for their journeys.

That they did not find themselves stranded and penniless in some out-of-the-way place.

It had all been very exciting.

Looking back, she felt she must complete her father's book, which he had not finished.

She should also contribute some interesting reminiscences of her own.

When he had died unexpectedly three weeks ago, without seeming to incur any specific illness, she was not only alone.

She had lost everything that was secure and understandable in her life.

It had never struck her father that, as she was nearly nineteen, she should be meeting men and women of her own age, especially the former.

They had been living for a little over a year in Devonshire.

The few friends they had made had looked at Zenobia, then stared as if they could not believe their eyes.

She was so unselfconscious that she was genuinely surprised when her father said to her:

"You are very lovely, my dearest, like your mother, and I sometimes think that all the beautiful places we have visited since we left England are mirrored in your face."

"That is a wonderful thing to say, Papa!" Zenobia replied.

When she was in her bedroom that night she had stared at herself in the mirror.

She hoped he was right.

She had lived for so long in India and other Eastern countries.

There the women with their huge dark eyes and coffee-coloured skins were so beautiful and at the same time different from herself.

It had never struck her that she was lovely too.

Now she saw her deep blue eyes, the colour of a stormy sea, dominating a heart-shaped face.

Her hair was the pale gold of early dawn.

She thought perhaps she did look a little like her mother.

If not beautiful, she was at least very pretty.

But that, she knew, was the wrong word.

"Pretty" implied the pink-and-white attractiveness of a typical English girl, to whom she bore little resemblance.

Her features were classical from her small, straight nose to the firm line of her chin.

Her lips might have been sculpted by Michelangelo.

The same applied to her body, which was that of a Greek goddess.

She did not, of course, think of herself in those terms.

She only thought that her eyes had a depth and mystery about them.

This she was sure was the result of probing deeply into the uncharted mysticism they had found in India.

In other lands they had sometimes encountered dangers which had nearly cost them their lives.

"What shall I do without Papa?" she had asked herself.

She had found him quietly asleep, his eyes closed, a faint smile on his lips.

He looked as if he were happy.

She was sure that in leaving this life he had found her mother again.

He had loved her with what was "one point" concentration from the first moment he had seen her.

It had been a crazy act on his part to marry again.

As she grew older, Zenobia had come to understand it was because he could not stand the loneliness or live in a house where the rooms were empty and the nights when he slept alone.

He had, in fact, been very vulnerable.

He was stricken and bewildered by the loss of the woman who held his heart.

Then, on a ship bringing him back from Egypt, he had met Irene.

She was in every way the exact opposite, Zenobia knew when she met her, from what her mother had been.

Very attractive—"fascinating" was the right word—she would look at a man from under her mascaraed eye-lashes flirtatiously.

She would make him feel she had something unusual about her that he must possess.

The widow of a soldier who had died fighting for his country, Irene was ready to console herself with every man she met.

It was by sheer chance that Lord Chadwell caught the ship at Alexandria only a few minutes before it sailed.

Irene was standing on deck when he was the last passenger up the gangway.

She thought he was extremely distinguished.

He was what she was looking for, a man alone with no encumbrances.

She learnt who he was from the Purser.

He also informed her that Lord Chadwell was rich and had recently become a widower.

Irene lost no time.

She attached herself to Lord Chadwell, and it would have been very difficult for him to rid himself of her.

He had spent the last few months alone in the desert with only the camelmen to talk to.

He was therefore glad of her company.

By the time they reached England, Irene had contrived that he was not only her lover, he had also asked her to marry him.

She enticed him cleverly and with an expertise which most men would have found irresistible.

Lord Chadwell had hardly known what was happening.

Suddenly he found himself married.

He bought, because it was Irene's wish, a large house in the fashionable part of London.

He had already given instructions before leaving for Egypt that the house in the country he had shared with his wife should be sold.

He could not bear to be haunted in every room by the memory of his happiness with Elizabeth.

He had sent Zenobia to live with her grandmother.

As soon as he returned, he wanted to see her again.

He was, however, frightened, although he would never have admitted it, that the very sight of the child would be too agonising to endure.

In fact, he had found himself happy in her company in a way he had not known since her mother's death.

He took her to the large house he had just bought in Park Street.

He knew that, if he had waited, he would have been content just to have Zenobia with him.

Then there would have been no need for him to marry Irene, but it was too late.

She immediately filled the house and his life with the social personalities she had always longed to know.

Everything was made easy now that she was Lady Chadwell.

Her husband belonged to an ancient family.

The members of which had served their country through every generation.

At first, because it was all new, Lord Chadwell had found it interesting to meet English people.

To hear their opinions, and add to his already vast knowledge of the human race.

But as dinner-party followed dinner-party, and he escorted his wife from one Ballroom to another, he was bored.

He found the conversation of the aristocrats they entertained was monotonous.

He started to feel restless.

He had been utterly content with Elizabeth because they loved each other so deeply.

They lived in the country with their horses and their dogs.

They explored the world through books rather than actively.

Elizabeth had never been strong.

They had visited parts of Europe, enjoying holidays in Majorca and Algiers.

Their love was complete and satisfying because they were together.

Their brains complemented each other's.

Lord Chadwell soon discovered that Irene's thoughts were as predictable and stereotyped as her love-making.

He gradually began to detach himself from the endless round of parties.

Perhaps it was inevitable, in the circumstances, that Irene took a lover.

Finding her husband was unaware of it, she had no compunction in taking another.

Lord Chadwell had been blind at first to what was happening.

When he did discover it, he was neither horrified nor enraged.

He was merely aware that his marriage had come to an end.

He had no intention of playing the part of a jealous husband.

Nor would he challenge the man concerned and fight what would be an illegal duel.

He knew that would be expected of him.

Although frowned on by Queen Victoria, duels still took place in Green Park at dawn.

If anybody was seriously injured or killed, the culprit had to leave the country.

Lord Chadwell thought it over.

He decided that without a duel and without any fuss he would simply leave England.

He had, though, no intention of going without his daughter.

He told the Nurse who looked after her that he was taking Zenobia to the country to stay with one of his relatives.

She was to pack everything the child needed.

"Will she be long away, M'Lord?" the Nurse enquired.

Lord Chadwell shrugged his shoulders.

"Perhaps a few weeks. Send her with enough clothes for every eventuality, a warm coat, and sensible shoes."

"Very good, M'Lord."

When Irene learned they were going away, she was not in the least concerned.

In fact, she thought it an excellent opportunity to enjoy herself with her latest lover.

She need not be afraid that her husband might discover them.

"I know you love the country, dearest," she said in her most beguiling voice, "but of course I shall miss you."

"I doubt it!" Lord Chadwell remarked dryly.

But she was not listening.

He and Zenobia left early in the morning before Irene was called.

There were therefore no fond good-byes nor any need to tell more lies than he had already.

They drove straight to Victoria Station.

Only when the train had started did Zenobia say:

"It is exciting to be going away with you, Papa! Where are we staying?"

"To-night we shall be on board a Liner sailing for India!" he replied.

For a moment she stared at him.

She was looking very childlike in an attractive coat which matched the colour of her eyes.

A round straw hat on the back of her head which looked like a halo.

Then she gave a cry of sheer joy and flung herself against her father.

"You are taking me to India?" she asked. "I cannot believe it! Oh, Papa, it will be wonderful to be there with you!"

She had in fact known a great deal more about her father's life and Irene's behaviour than anybody would have expected.

Servants invariably talk in front of children as if they are deaf.

She had heard her Nurse and the Housekeeper when they thought she was asleep shaking their heads over Irene and saying:

"It's a real shame, that's what it is!"

"What can she see in 'em when the Master's such a pleasant gentleman?"

She also knew that the old servants who had loved her mother thought Irene was not worthy of her father.

They always spoke of her as "a poor motherless child."

They were thinking she knew of how inadequately Irene filled the place of her real mother.

From that moment of their journey Zenobia was rapturously happy.

Her love for her father deepened every year that they were together.

Only after his Funeral did she begin to think about her future.

"What shall I do?" she asked.

The local Solicitor in the nearby town had helped her father buy their house.

He was the only person she could ask for advice.

He helped her look through her father's papers.

They found a Will dated soon after she and her father had left England.

It had been registered by an Indian lawyer in Calcutta.

It was very short and it merely stated:

*In the event of my death, I leave everything
I possess to my daughter, Zenobia Chade.*

In the letter that accompanied it from the Indian official was the information that he had sent a copy to her father's Solicitors, Burke, Powell, and Burke, in London.

"They will help you, Miss Zenobia," the Solicitor said, "and the best thing you can do is to get in touch with them."

"As I have a great deal to do here before I leave," Zenobia said, "perhaps you would be kind enough to do that for me?"

Mr. Bushell appeared embarrassed.

Then, as if he thought it best to be honest, he replied:

"You must be aware, Miss Zenobia, that you cannot, at your age, live alone."

"To tell you the truth, I have never thought about it," Zenobia said. "I have always been with Papa, and was so happy with him that I have no idea now where I can go, or indeed if I have any relatives alive."

"You must have some!" Mr. Bushell exclaimed.

"I know both my grandmothers are now dead," Zenobia replied, "and Papa was not interested in any of the others, if indeed any exist!"

She gave a deep sigh.

"We had been abroad for so long before we came here that I am quite sure he had forgotten about them, except I suppose the cousin he never liked who will inherit his title."

"But you cannot live alone!" Mr. Bushell said firmly. "And if the house in Park Street is yours, I am sure it would be more accommodating for you to stay there than anywhere else."

Zenobia did not argue.

Like her father, she found it tedious to disagree with people, especially when they were trying to be kind.

She told Mr. Bushell to put the house in Devonshire in which they had been living up for sale.

She knew that, like her father after her mother's death, she could not bear to live in it now that he was gone.

Anyway, it had never seemed like a real home.

As soon as his book was finished they had intended to go abroad again.

Neither she nor her father believed in death.

The body wore out like an old suit of clothes, but the spirit was very much alive.

Zenobia therefore made no pretence of wearing black.

She had few clothes, all of them very simple and easy to pack.

Both she and her father liked to travel light.

12

She seldom had more than two or three gowns at a time.

She wore them hard, and discarded them when they were worn out.

What she had to pack was therefore very little in the matter of clothes.

Her father's books were a different matter.

He had accumulated a great number, even in the year they had been in Devonshire.

Zenobia, however, packed them all up and took them with her to London.

All through the long journey she was wondering what she would do or where she could go.

She was quite certain of one thing:

She would not stay in a house with her Stepmother.

She supposed it would take some time for Irene to move out of the big house in which she had lived for the last thirteen years.

She wondered if she had changed much.

It was difficult to remember what she looked like when she last saw her.

Zenobia could remember the scent of the exotic perfume Irene had used, the jewels with which she adorned herself.

Her gowns that always seemed to glitter.

When she moved she shimmered with the seductive movements of a snake.

Zenobia calculated that Irene was now well over forty.

Perhaps she was no longer so obsessed with the Social World, as she had been in the past.

When Zenobia arrived at Paddington a porter collected her trunk and the large crate of books from the Guard's Van.

He found her a Hackney carriage which would take her to Park Street.

She had already written to Irene to say that she was coming to London.

There had been no reply, and she had not really expected one.

She had announced her father's death in *The Times* and the *Morning Post*.

She supposed that even before she received her letter, Irene had learnt that she was again a widow.

The house in Park Street did not look very large or impressive.

Which was what it had seemed to her when she was a child.

There was a Butler and two footmen wearing the Chadwell livery in the hall.

When she said who she was, the Butler took her upstairs to the *Boudoir* which adjoined Irene's bedroom.

It was just as Zenobia expected it to be.

It was filled with a large amount of hot-house flowers whose fragrance pervaded the room.

Besides the gilded and richly brocaded furniture, there was a profusion of small tables.

They contained knick-knacks and *objets d'art*.

A flowered screen of peacocks' feathers was rivalled by huge aspidistras in Chinese pots.

As it was six o'clock in the evening, Irene was reclining on a *chaise longue*.

Her head was resting against a satin cushion.

It was the time of day at which Zenobia remembered she usually entertained some elegant young man.

Her Nurse had always been instructed to keep her out of the way on no account was she to disturb her Stepmother.

Now Irene was alone.

Lying back with her feet covered by an ermine rug, she watched Zenobia approach her.

There was a hard expression in her dark eyes.

"Good-evening, Stepmama!" Zenobia said politely. "I hope you received my letter."

"I got it!" Irene replied. "But if you have come here to make trouble, you have had a wasted journey!"

Zenobia raised her eye-brows.

As Irene did not invite her to sit down, she chose a chair near to the *chaise longue*.

"I have no desire to make trouble," she said in her soft voice, "but I am afraid Papa was very negligent over his monetary affairs and had no idea that he might die. I have therefore come to London to discover what my position is."

Irene did not reply and Zenobia went on:

"Papa made a Will leaving me everything he possessed, and that of course includes this house and its contents, and I imagine what money he had in the Bank."

Irene gave a little laugh which had no humour in it.

"You are certainly deluding yourself if you think your father had anything to leave you apart from this house!"

"What do you mean?" Zenobia enquired.

"I mean that what money he had has all been spent except for a few hundred pounds, and I think my claim on that for my living expenses would, in a Court of Law, be stronger than yours!"

"I do not know what you are saying!" Zenobia exclaimed.

"Then let me make it clearer," Irene replied in a hard voice. "Your father left me without a word in what I consider was an insulting manner. Fortunately, however, he had arranged when we married that I would draw on his account at Coutts Bank."

There was a little pause, then Zenobia asked incredulously:

"Are you telling me that you have spent . . . everything he . . . possessed?"

"To put it bluntly—yes!" Irene replied. "Even so, I can assure you I should have been hard pressed for money if I had not had some very kind and generous *friends!*"

She emphasised the last word, which made it very clear to Zenobia what she meant.

She could not help giving a little shiver of revulsion.

Then she said, and her voice was quite calm:

"I always understood that Papa was a very rich man and that his money was well invested."

"Then you understood wrong!" Irene said spitefully. "I reinvested some of his money, but the old-fashioned stocks he held paid very small dividends and, quite frankly, it was his duty as my husband to keep me in comfort."

"In other words, you have spent the capital as well as the income!" Zenobia said. "I am only surprised that neither you nor the Bank informed Papa of what you were doing!"

"It was hardly possible when none of us had any idea of where you were!" Irene snapped.

Zenobia had to admit that was true.

Her father had cut off all ties with England.

Yet there always seemed to be money when they needed it at the Bank nearest to where they were living.

Neither he nor she had ever thought that the money might dry up or that Irene would be over-spending.

Shocked and disturbed by what she had heard, Zenobia did not speak for a moment.

Until she said:

"There is of course this house!"

"I mortgaged it!" Irene retorted.

"Mortgaged it?"

"I needed more money, and it seemed the most sensible thing to do."

"But it now belongs to me!" Zenobia murmured.

"A lot of good it will do you without the money to keep it up," Irene said. "And if you do claim it, the Bank will presumably expect the money they have advanced to be returned to them as soon as possible!"

Zenobia suddenly felt helpless.

But she lifted her chin proudly as she said:

"You must be aware, Stepmama, that I have to live!"

"I cannot see why!" Irene answered nastily. "However, as I presume I am your Guardian until you are twenty-one, I suppose I had better find you a husband as quickly as possible, and get you off my hands."

This was something that had never entered Zenobia's mind.

In a low voice she said:

"I never . . . thought of you as . . . being my . . . Guardian."

"That is what I am in the eyes of the Law!" Irene replied. "There are therefore two things I can do. One would be to disown you, which might cause something of a scandal."

She spoke the words reluctantly.

Zenobia knew the one thing she did not want was any gossip of any sort.

That she had disowned Lord Chadwell's daughter would cause her to be censured by older people who remembered her father.

"The alternative," Irene went on, "is for you to stay here and make the best of it. I will, as I have said, try to find you a husband, which should not be difficult, as you are passably good-looking, and your mother was the daughter of an Earl."

Zenobia drew in her breath.

She knew that was the only reason why Irene, who had always been a snob, would tolerate her.

She would also make an effort to get her off her hands by marrying her to the first man who came along.

To Zenobia that idea was frightening and disgusting.

She wanted to rise from her chair, walk out of Irene's life, and never see her again.

Then the self-control she had learnt how to exercise with her father told her to do nothing foolish.

She thought she must play for time.

In a voice she strove not to sound sarcastic, she said:

"That is very kind of you, Stepmama, and it is certainly something I would like to consider, but as it is getting late, and I have nowhere else to go to-night, I hope I may stay here."

"You do not suppose any reputable Hotel would take you without a chaperone?" Irene sneered. "I have a dinner-party to-night, and I suppose you had better appear at it if you have anything decent to wear."

"As I have been travelling since very early this morning," Zenobia replied, "I hope you will forgive me if I go to bed. All the same, thank you for thinking of it."

She saw the relief on Irene's face.

She reached out to ring the little gold bell that stood beside her *chaise longue*.

The door opened.

A woman who Zenobia guessed was a lady's-maid asked:

"You rang, M'Lady?"

"Yes, Johnson. Take Miss Zenobia to the room I had prepared for her, and see that the footmen bring up her luggage."

Irene spoke sharply.

It was a way in which Zenobia remembered she always spoke to servants.

Without saying any more, she went from the room and followed the maid down the passage.

There was a room at the other end, which she knew was kept in the past for less important guests.

But it was quite comfortable.

The curtains were of a pretty chintz, but the carpet was a riot of colour.

Zenobia thought it was in rather bad taste.

Her trunks were brought upstairs, and a maid unpacked only what she needed for the night.

After a light supper she got into bed.

The servants, as she had somehow expected they would be, seemed surly.

She wondered what Irene had done with the old servants whom she remembered as a child.

When she was in bed, she lay wondering frantically what she should do and where she could go.

She could approach the Solicitors and call at the Bank to find out how much was really left to her.

She was sure if there was anything worth having, Irene would have got her hands on it.

All the time she had lived with her father they had always had what money they needed without their being any worry about it.

They had always employed a reasonable number of servants to look after them in India and other parts of the world.

Zenobia had however always thought that they were spending little compared to what her father would have spent in London.

She supposed they had been stupid not to have realised that Irene would be wildly extravagant.

Not only as regards her clothes, as she always had been, but also in her hospitality.

She had intended to become an important hostess.

Later Zenobia heard loud laughter from downstairs.

She wondered if "important" was the right word.

She had always known that Irene was not really well-bred or from a good family background.

She suspected that the more distinguished hostesses in London, and the exclusive "Marlborough House Set" would have little to do with her.

"I will find out more to-morrow," she promised herself.

Then she knew there was no point if she was not going to live here.

But where could she live? Where else could she go?

Although she was tired, it was impossible to sleep.

She tossed and turned until she heard the guests leaving. Their voices and laughter came up from the hall.

There was the noise of carriages driving away outside.

She hoped that once the house was quiet she would be able to sleep.

*　　*　　*

It was a little later when she realised she felt thirsty.

She got up and went to the wash-hand-stand which stood in a corner of the room.

The carafe for drinking-water was empty.

It was a bad oversight on the part of the Housekeeper who had prepared the room for her.

Then she thought she might find some drinking-water next door.

It was, she remembered, a large double room.

She supposed it to be empty.

She opened her bedroom door to find that the lights in the passage had been partially extinguished.

She could however see her way clearly enough.

Wearing a dressing-gown but with bare feet, she went into the next room.

By leaving the door open she could see her way to the wash-hand-stand.

Now she was rewarded with a full carafe, although she suspected it had not been recently re-filled.

She drank thirstily.

Then she filled the glass again, and carrying it in her hand, started to return to her own room.

As she was about to step into the corridor, she was aware that two people were coming up the stairs.

Surprised, she hastily stepped back.

As they passed she saw it was Irene.

There was no mistaking the scent of expensive French perfume she left behind as she went down the passage.

The man walking with her had his arm around her waist.

They disappeared through the door of Irene's bedroom.

Zenobia felt a shiver of revulsion.

It was not that she was surprised; it was rather that it was intolerable to think that this immoral woman had been the wife of her father.

What was even worse, she was her Guardian.

When Zenobia went back into her own bedroom, she knew one thing very clearly.

If it meant she had to starve in the gutter, she would not stay under the same roof as Irene for one moment longer than was absolutely necessary.

chapter two

ZENOBIA slept very little.

When morning came, a plan had formed in her mind.

She rang her bell much earlier than anyone might have expected.

The elderly housemaid who had attended to her when she arrived came hurrying into the rome.

She was obviously surprised that she was awake.

Zenobia said she wanted to get up.

A message was sent downstairs for breakfast to be readied for her.

Then as the housemaid started to help her dress she asked:

"Have you been here long? I was hoping that perhaps I would find some of the old servants who were here when my father lived here."

"Oh, no, Miss!" the housemaid replied. "I think they left years ago!"

There was a little pause, then she added:

"An' I won't be here much longer!"

"Why not?" Zenobia asked.

"Too many late nights, Miss. The last place I were in, with Lady Marchmont, we never 'ad late nights like this, but then, unfortunately, the Lady died."

"That was sad," Zenobia said, "and how did you find another place?"

"The same way as we all does," the housemaid answered. "I went to Mrs. Dawson's in Mount Street, who's got the best Domestic Agency in London. She found me this position an' I 'opes she soon finds me another."

Zenobia had learnt what she wanted to know.

After breakfast she put on her hat and a light jacket and went down the stairs.

She knew her Stepmother had not been called.

Seeing her alone, the footman looked surprised as he opened the front-door.

In case there were any questions asked, she said:

"I am not going far, only round to the Grosvenor Chapel, so there is no need for anybody to accompany me."

He grinned at her in a friendly way.

Zenobia hurried off; it was unlikely her Stepmother would expect to see her for at least two hours.

She found her way to Mount Street.

She discovered the Agency was on the First Floor over a shop.

When she entered, it was to find a large room with a number of servants sitting on a bench near the door.

At the far end there was a high desk at which an elderly woman was writing in a ledger.

There was a middle-aged woman beside her, who looked harassed.

It was as if the effort of pleasing her employer and the applicants for the available jobs were very exhausting.

Both women looked at Zenobia as she entered.

The younger of the two came hurrying towards her to say:

"What can we do for you, Ma'am?"

Zenobia realised that they thought she had come to engage a servant.

In what she hoped was a confident manner she said:

"I am hoping that Mrs. Dawson can find me a position as a secretary."

"A secretary?" the woman exclaimed.

She was obviously surprised.

Before she could say any more, however, Zenobia walked determinedly up to the desk.

"How do you do?" she said. "I have heard glowing accounts of your Agency, Mrs. Dawson, which is why I have come here."

She held out her hand as she spoke.

Somewhat reluctantly, the old woman shook hands with her.

"She's asking for a position as a secretary!" the other woman interposed.

Mrs. Dawson scrutinised Zenobia from over her spectacles.

Then in an uncompromising voice she enquired:

"Have you got any qualifications?"

From the way she spoke it was obvious she thought these were non-existent.

Zenobia, refusing to be intimidated, said quietly:

"I speak fluently a number of foreign languages, including French, Italian, and Spanish, some Hungarian and a little Arabic."

Both women stared at her, and Mrs. Dawson said:

"Have you references to prove this?"

Zenobia had already thought what she should reply to this inevitable but awkward question.

She answered quietly:

"Unfortunately my last employer, Lord Chadwell, with whom I travelled a great deal, died unexpectedly a few weeks ago, and as I had no intention of leaving him, it had never occurred to me to ask him for a reference."

"That is certainly unfortunate!" Mrs. Dawson agreed.

"I am prepared to submit to any test to prove that I am not exaggerating my capabilities," Zenobia said, "and as Lord Chadwell was writing a book of his experiences, I am used to taking down dictation at quite a fast speed."

Mrs. Dawson turned over the pages of her ledger.

"We've got a large number of applicants," she said slowly, "for both indoor and outdoor servants, but secretaries are in any case usually men."

She turned another two pages and went on:

"There are ladies who would be prepared to take on a woman more or less as a companion, but even they wouldn't consider taking anyone as young as you obviously are."

She picked up her quill pen and added:

"You can give me your name, but I will be frank and say it's very unlikely that I will be able to accommodate you."

"My name is Webb."

Zenobia had chosen the surname "Webb" because it had belonged to one of her Governesses.

She was the only one who had taught her English, and of whom she had been very fond.

Mrs. Dawson inscribed the name in her ledger.

Zenobia realised the interview was finished. Then she heard the other woman whisper something in Mrs. Dawson's ear.

Her voice was low, but Zenobia heard her say quite distinctly:

"What about the Earl of Ockendon?"

Mrs. Dawson looked at her assistant with raised eyebrows.

"He definitely wants a man!"

"It seems unlikely he'll find one," the assistant answered, "especially someone who speaks Eastern languages."

"If you are talking about the East," Zenobia interposed, "I have lived in India for quite some time, so I can speak *Urdu*, and I have also been in Ceylon and other countries in that part of the world."

"Well, that's certainly unusual!" Mrs. Dawson exclaimed.

She turned her head to whisper to her assistant.

Now she covered one side of her face with her raised hand.

She wanted to make quite certain that Zenobia could not hear what they were saying.

Because she had no wish to eaves-drop, she moved a little way from the desk.

She looked at the people waiting.

It was quite obvious that three of the men were grooms and two of the women, she guessed, were experienced housemaids.

There were also several quite young, apple-cheeked girls.

They had obviously come up from the country in search of work.

While she was looking she was saying a little prayer that she might find what she wanted.

Any place, she thought, would be better than staying in the same house with her Stepmother.

She would be forced to meet her friends, who doubtless were as immoral and unprincipled as she was.

Mrs. Dawson had obviously made up her mind, for she now said:

"I have a client, Miss Webb, who is enquiring for a male secretary, but who may, in the circumstances, if you have told me the truth, be prepared to give you a try."

"I will certainly do my best to please," Zenobia murmured.

"I think it's unlikely," Mrs. Dawson went on grudgingly, "that the Earl of Ockendon would consider you for the position that is open at the moment."

She paused to go on grudgingly:

"But His Lordship's in a hurry, and we have unfortunately no one else to send him who is at all proficient in languages, either European or Eastern."

Zenobia did not speak, but she felt a little quiver of hope.

Mrs. Dawson wrote an address on one of her printed cards and handed it to her.

"Take this to Ockendon House, which is Number twenty-seven, Park Lane," she said, "and if His Lordship hasn't yet found somebody satisfactory, you might have a chance. If he refuses to engage you, you can come back here. But I think you must be prepared to consider a different sort of employment."

"Thank you very much," Zenobia said, "I am very grateful to you."

She put the card into her hand-bag, smiled at Mrs. Dawson, and walked from the room.

She was well aware as she left that the two elderly women were quite sure it was a waste of time.

She had no chance whatsoever of pleasing the Earl of Ockendon, whoever he might be.

It was a short distance from Mount Street to Park Lane, and the Earl's house was easy to find.

It was on the corner of South Street, overlooking the Park.

It stood back from the road with a drive in and, Zenobia guessed, a garden at the rear.

It was many years since she had last been in London.

But she could still remember the beauty of Hyde Park, where she had been taken for walks by her Nurse.

The tall houses in Park Lane which had always seemed to her like Palaces were still there.

Her father had sometimes talked about London.

He told her how he had enjoyed the gaiety of it as a young man, until he had retired to the country with her mother.

Zenobia knew they had been blissfully happy until her death.

She thought now that Ockendon House was exactly the right sort of background for her father.

It would have suited his tall figure and distinguished looks.

Then she remembered that ever since his marriage to Irene, he had hated London.

Her endless search for pleasure had resulted in her taking one lover after another.

'I would actually prefer to be in the country,' Zenobia thought, 'but perhaps the Earl is an old man, and needs to be near his doctors.'

She had assumed that no young man would be interested, as her father had been, in strange languages and distant countries.

She imagined that the Earl was perhaps writing his memoirs.

It would be after a long life of service to the Queen.

She rang the bell.

When the door was opened by a footman she showed him Mrs. Dawson's card and said:

"I have been sent by Mrs. Dawson in answer to the Earl of Ockendon's request for a secretary."

She thought the young man stared at her in surprise.

He hurried to the end of the hall.

A Butler with white hair and a pontifical manner was just emerging from a passage which Zenobia guessed led to the Pantry.

He looked at the card carefully.

Zenobia stood waiting just inside the front-door.

Then he came towards her and said:

"Do I understand, Miss, that you are applying for the position of secretary to His Lordship?"

His voice sounded so incredulous that Zenobia almost laughed.

Controlling herself, she replied:

"That is why I am here, and I shall be grateful if it is possible to see His Lordship."

The Butler looked at her as if she had made a social gaffe.

In a reproving voice he replied:

"I will take you to Mr. Williamson."

He moved away down a passage from the opposite side of the hall without waiting for her.

She thought the name "Williamson" sounded like that of a secretary.

She wondered why, if His Lordship already had a secretary, he should want another.

They walked for quite a little way before the Butler opened a door.

Zenobia saw at a glance the room was an office.

Sitting at a desk was a man with greying hair who looked up impatiently as the Butler entered.

"What is it, Bateson?" he enquired.

"And applicant for the secretarial post, Sir," the Butler replied, "who's come from Mrs. Dawson."

As he spoke he handed the card to Mr. Williamson, who looked first at Zenobia.

Then he stared at the card.

As the Butler withdrew, Zenobia walked forward and held out her hand.

"It is obvious," she said, "that everybody is surprised that I should be here, being a woman! But I do speak quite a number of both European and Eastern languages."

Her quiet, cultured voice obviously impressed Mr. Williamson.

He made a gesture as if to rise from his seat before he said:

"Will you sit down, and tell me how it is possible for anyone who looks so young to be proficient in a large number of languages?"

He paused for a moment. Then he said:

"Perhaps you should first tell me your name."

"It is Webb," Zenobia replied briefly.

"I do not know whether Mrs. Dawson has explained to you why His Lordship needs a secretary?"

"I was thinking that it seemed strange when he already had you," Zenobia replied.

"It is true that I am his secretary," Mr. Williamson replied, "but I manage His Lordship's houses and make his engagements. What he needs at the moment is somebody to help him with the Colonial and Indian Exhibition which will be held in the Royal Albert Hall next year."

Zenobia gave a little exclamation.

"Another Exhibition? I understand there have been several in the past!"

She remembered, as she spoke, a luncheon she and her father had enjoyed in India.

Their host, a Maharajah, had expressed his regret that he was unable to show them an ivory elephant studded with precious stones.

He had sent it to England to be shown at an Exhibition that was taking place there in 1880.

"I see you are well informed, Miss Webb," Mr. Williamson was saying, "but this Exhibition is to be on a grander scale than any of those which have taken place before. In fact, His Lordship has been particularly asked by Her Majesty the Queen to make sure that both India and our Colonies are properly represented."

"I understand," Zenobia replied.

She was thinking as she spoke that it was something she might have thought of herself.

"As the Exhibition is to be opened on May first next year, His Lordship has only a short time in which to request and obtain the loan of the Exhibits he wants. He thinks it important also that he should write to the owners in their own languages."

"That is very sensible," Zenobia agreed.

She knew how long it took to get letters translated.

Often, because they were done by somebody not fully experienced in English, misunderstandings had occurred, leading inevitably to long delays.

"At the same time," Mr. Williamson was saying, "although you may be proficient, as you say you are, Miss Webb, I think you are too young for this particular post."

"I cannot really see what age has to do with it," Zenobia objected. "After all, I have lived in India, I speak Urdu fluently and Singhalese quite well. I can also make myself understood in Singapore."

"It does not seem possible," Mr. Williamson murmured,

"but there are other reasons why, as a family man, I think you would be wise to look elsewhere for employment."

Zenobia looked puzzled.

She felt from the way Mr. Williamson was talking that there was some mystery about the Earl.

At the same time, he was, although it seemed strange, trying to be kind to her.

"You are very considerate," she said after a little pause, "but I am very anxious, if it is possible, to have this position, first because I know it will interest me, and secondly because I need to leave where I am at present as quickly as possible."

As she spoke she thought perhaps she had said the wrong thing and added:

"It is not that I am employed there, but that I am unhappy with the relations with whom I am staying."

"And I presume also you need the money?" Mr. Williamson said.

"Of course!" Zenobia agreed.

"Very well, I will take you to see His Lordship, but obviously the decision is his."

Zenobia smiled.

"If I get the position, Mr. Williamson, I shall be very grateful, and then perhaps you will warn me of all the pitfalls so that I can walk carefully and not make too many mistakes."

As she spoke she knew that was not what he had been thinking about.

Yet why had he said she would do better to look elsewhere?

Mr. Williamson rose and said:

"I will go and speak to His Lordship. I do not suppose that anybody has told you he has had an accident to his leg, which has for the moment incapacitated him, and the doctors have advised him to move about as little as possible."

Mr. Williamson went towards the door, and as he reached it he looked back.

Zenobia could see there was a very worried expression on his face.

"I wonder what is wrong?" she asked herself.

She thought it was rather intriguing.

Because she had been so long in the East, she had developed an extraordinarily strong perception about people.

In fact, she had often thought that at times she could read their thoughts.

Her father used to laugh at her.

He would say she was boasting of magical powers she did not in fact possess.

When they had been in danger, however, she had always seemed to sense it before it actually took place.

Also she was invariably aware when people they were meeting were hostile before they revealed their true feelings.

"Why should he be so worried?" she asked.

Then she thought he might be away for some time.

She rose from the chair and walked to the window.

She had been right in guessing there was a garden at the rear of the house.

It was very small, but the flower-beds were bright with bedded-out plants.

The leaves on the trees were the pale green of spring.

They made her long for the beauty she had left behind in Devonshire.

She had what was an emotional craving for the wildness of the undulating land above the cliffs, the taste of salt in the air.

"Oh, Papa," she asked in her heart, "why did you have

to die? And how could I ever have imagined that there would be no money and it would be a question of either living with Irene or of earning my own living?"

She had the feeling that her father would wish her to earn her own living.

He had seldom spoken of the wife he had deserted.

When he did, there was a note in his voice which told his daughter all too clearly how much he despised her.

He had never forgotten the way she had dishonoured his name.

She was thinking of her father, when the door opened and Mr. Williamson came back.

"I have explained to His Lordship about you, Miss Webb," he said, "and because we have been very disappointed up to date with those who have applied for the position as secretary, His Lordship will see you. I only hope you have not exaggerated your talents."

Zenobia laughed, and it was a happy sound.

"In that case, His Lordship will be angry with you, Mr. Williamson! But I can set your mind at rest and promise you I am telling the truth."

As if he dared not be too optimistic, Mr. Williamson led Zenobia up the stairs in silence.

As he opened a door at the end of a long corridor, she felt he was more worried than ever.

"Miss Webb, My Lord!" he announced.

As Zenobia walked forward, she saw the Earl of Ockendon.

He was sitting in the window, partially dressed, with his injured leg on a stool.

He was not in the least what she had expected.

Far from being elderly, he was a man she guessed to be about thirty years old.

He was broad-shouldered and exceedingly handsome.

Because she was so surprised, it took her a second before she remembered to curtsy.

Then she walked forward respectfully.

He looked at her.

Although Mr. Williamson must have told him that she looked very young, there was an unmistakable expression of surprise in his eyes.

Actually, while Mr. Williamson had emphasised that she was very young, he had omitted to tell his employer that Zenobia was very lovely.

With the sunshine coming through the window, on her clear, almost translucent skin.

With her unusually deep blue eyes and heart-shaped face, she was in no way what the Earl had expected.

The sun seemed also to accentuate the gold of her hair.

After he had looked at her for what seemed a long time, he asked sharply:

"Is this a joke?"

"A joke?" Zenobia questioned.

"I presume somebody has been talking to you about my need of a secretary for the Exhibition," the Earl said sharply, "and you thought it would be amusing to try to deceive me!"

"I promise you I am doing no such thing!" Zenobia replied. "Your secretary, Mr. Williamson, doubted the truth of what I told him of my capabilities, but I can only repeat that I do speak the languages you require."

She thought he was still incredulous, and after a moment she added:

"Please let me help you with the Exhibition! It is something I would enjoy enormously, and as I have been to most of the places whose products you will exhibit, I am sure I will be able to help you."

The Earl gave a short laugh that had no humour in it.

"You are very plausible, Miss Webb!" he said. "But I am still extremely suspicious."

Zenobia made a little gesture with her hands.

"How can I convince you that I am what I say I am?" She asked the question in Urdu.

After a moment's hesitation the Earl replied:

"I suppose, in the circumstances, I will have to trust you."

"I hope you will do that because it is important to me," Zenobia answered, and now she spoke in Singhalese.

The Earl laughed again, but this time it was a genuine sound.

"You win, Miss Webb!" he said. "Sit down and tell me about yourself."

Zenobia chose a chair that was near him.

Then as she was aware he was waiting she said:

"As I have already told Mr. Williamson, I was employed by the late Lord Chadwell, who was a great traveller."

"Employed? For how many years?" the Earl asked.

Zenobia had already decided that she would pretend to be older than she really was, and she replied:

"Five . . . nearly six years."

The Earl did not speak.

She knew he was calculating that if she was eighteen when she first entered Lord Chadwell's service, she must now be twenty-three.

She realised he was wondering if that was possible.

She lifted her chin a little as she said:

"I have already said once to-day that I cannot see why age should have anything to do with my ability to speak languages."

He did not reply and she went on:

"What is important is that I know India quite well, and I

have visited a great number of our Colonies, including Ceylon, many in Africa, and our Mediterranean possessions."

"I suppose I shall have to believe you," the Earl said, "but I would like to make it quite clear, Miss Webb, that if you do not live up to your own estimation of yourself, I shall not hesitate to dismiss you and try, although I admit it seems to be difficult, to find somebody else."

"I only hope, My Lord, that you will not be disappointed," Zenobia answered.

"Very well," the Earl said, "when can you start? As it happens, I am leaving for the country to-morrow, as I feel I shall get better more quickly in the fresh air than I will staying in London."

"I am glad about that," Zenobia said involuntarily.

She spoke with such enthusiasm that the Earl looked at her in surprise.

"I thought all young women liked London," he said with a cynical note in his voice.

"I do not know it well, but what I do know about it I dislike!" Zenobia answered.

She thought of her Stepmother as she spoke.

She had no idea that the expression on her face was very revealing.

"I am going to Ockendon Castle which, as I expect you know, is in Buckinghamshire," the Earl informed her.

"I must tell you honestly I had never heard of you until your name was mentioned by Mrs. Dawson, but it will be very exciting to see one of Britain's ancestral homes, which I have always heard are very magnificent!"

Only after she had said it did she feel that she had spoken to the Earl as if she were an equal rather than a servant.

She added quickly:

"I am hoping, My Lord, that my work will give you satisfaction, wherever we may be."

"That remains to be seen!" the Earl said. "As I shall be leaving early in the morning, and so will my household, in my private train, I suggest you meet us at Paddington Station at nine o'clock. If you are late, we shall, of course, leave without you!"

"I shall not be late, My Lord," Zenobia replied, "and thank you very much for employing me."

She rose as she spoke and made him a graceful cursty.

She walked towards the door, leaving the room without looking back.

The Earl stared after her and after a moment said beneath his breath:

"Now, what the devil is all this about, and who is she?"

* * *

When Mr. Williamson came back to the room a little later, he repeated the same words.

Mr. Williamson, having given Zenobia precise instructions and seen her off, now returned somewhat anxiously to his master's bedroom.

"I thought at first somebody was playing a joke on me," the Earl said, "but she speaks Urdu well, as far as I can tell, though I am not proficient in that language, and Singhalese too!"

"I am sure she is too young for the post, Your Lordship," Mr. Williamson said.

The Earl's eyes twinkled.

"I know exactly what you are thinking, Williamson, but she seems a very self-possessed young woman, although doubtless she will make a nuisance of herself!"

The way the Earl spoke was somewhat scathing.

There was however a twinkle in his eyes and a twist to his lips.

No one knew better than he did how when women fell in love with him they became a nuisance.

It usually meant tears and recriminations when they were dispensed with.

He knew his secretary was thinking at the moment of a Nurse.

She had been sent to look after him by the doctors.

She was an experienced, well-trained woman of over thirty, but she had fallen madly in love with her patient.

The Earl had said irritably that he was sick to death of her mooning over him and making unnecessary excuses to touch him.

She had left in floods of tears, declaring to all and sundry that her heart was broken.

Mr. Williamson knew that in that instance no possible blame could have been attached to the Earl.

He had been feeling far too ill and irritable to be interested even in the Venus de Milo.

But there had, in the past, been a large number of ladies and what the French called *"demi-mondaines"* with whom Mr. Williamson had been obliged to cope.

"I cannot understand why other men can have love-affairs without their being so much fuss about it!" the Earl had said once.

Mr. Williamson knew the answer to this.

The Earl was exceptional.

He was not only very handsome and an extremely fine sportsman, but he had something else.

It was that magnetic quality which occurs occasionally in both men and women and makes them irresistible to the opposite sex.

Women gravitated towards the Earl like flies round a honey-pot.

Even if he showed no interest in them, they still fawned on him.

They did everything in their power to attract him.

Where his *affaires de coeur* were concerned, he himself was only interested in the sophisticated, beautiful women with whom Society abounded.

The most lovely of them were known as "Professional Beauties" because their photographs appeared in every Stationer's window.

All the men of the *Beau Ton* were attracted by them.

The sensational Lillie Langtry, who was known as the "Jersey Lily," had captivated all London.

She had apparently possessed originally only one gown.

She was so exceedingly lovely that the Prince of Wales had fallen at her feet.

The Earl had won himself a name for finding women who were not acknowledged Beauties and making them spring overnight, as it were, to fame.

He had only to be seen at Covent Garden or at a party with a woman for everybody to ask immediately who she was.

By the following morning she would be spoken of as a Beauty.

The Earl had added another trophy to those he had already collected.

When Zenobia presented herself looking very lovely, although in a different way from the Professional Beauties, the Earl had strongly suspected that a joke was being played on him.

Or else she was yet another designing woman, trying to insinuate herself into his company.

At any other time he might have refused to step into what he thought must be a deliberately baited trap.

But he was desperate to find a secretary who could write letters to the countries concerned in the Exhibition.

He thought therefore the only thing he could do was to try her out and see if she was true or false.

It was the Queen herself who had spoken to him very earnestly about the Colonial and Indian Exhibition for next year.

"I have been a little disappointed at those that have taken place so far," she said. "I think of how much better dear Albert would have arranged them, just as he astounded the whole world by what he achieved in the Great Exhibition in the Crystal Palace."

He knew exactly what the Queen meant when she said that previous exhibitions had been somewhat "second-rate."

The exhibits were not always the finest the country from which they came could have provided.

"I am relying on you, My Lord," the Queen had said, "to make this Exhibition worthy of our Empire."

She did not add "and of me!" but the Earl knew that was what she was thinking.

"I will certainly do my very best, Ma'am," the Earl replied.

Because it was a Royal Command, he would have started to work on it right away had he not had an accident which had nearly shattered one of his legs.

It made him, to his fury, an invalid running for at least a month a high temperature.

Now he was better and he was determined that nothing should prevent him from going ahead with the Queen's request.

He had a year in which to do it: at the same time, he

was well aware the posts were not as efficient as they might be.

There would therefore be delays before his letters arrived.

Therefore, with many difficulties before certain objects he required were packed up, despatched, and arrived in England, the Exhibition would suffer.

No one before had ever been intelligent enough to write to the owners of the items desired in their own languages.

He was sure this would prove far more effective than requests to the Viceroy of India that he should approach the Maharajahs and Princes concerned, when he had other and more urgent duties.

The Earl had dismissed such a channel long ago as being laborious and too slow.

'I will make a success of this if it kills me!' he thought.

No one was more determined or self-willed than the Earl when he had a definite project on which to concentrate.

*   *   *

Returning to Chadwell House, Zenobia thought she had not only been clever, but also very lucky.

It seemed incredible that she had been fortunate enough to find a position which would take her away from her Stepmother.

It was also one she knew she would find absorbingly interesting.

She could understand that the Earl and Mr. Williamson thought it impossible for women to really be of any use.

Her father had often told he she was unique in being very much better educated than the average girl of her age.

"We English are extraordinary people," he had said. "We take a great amount of trouble to see that our sons are intelligent and educated, so that they can perform their future functions as leaders in Church and State."

"But what about an English gentleman's daughters?" Zenobia asked, knowing the answer.

"They are dragged up with only one idea, and that is to get married to the highest bidder," her father said scornfully. "They are taught the little they know by some plain woman who has been unable to find herself a husband and in most cases is almost as ignorant as her pupils!"

"That is very scathing, Papa!"

"You have never had to endure English Governesses because I took you away from all that nonsense."

"But surely men, when they marry, want their wives to be intelligent?" Zenobia asked.

"If they do, they are disappointed," her father said. "Your mother was different. She had a natural intelligence, and was a great reader."

"Yes, I know that," Zenobia murmured.

"She always admitted her Governesses had taught her nothing," Lord Chadwell went on, "but she read widely because she enjoyed it, and we studied together many subjects which I am now teaching you."

"That is what I enjoy, Papa," Zenobia said, "and have no wish to have any other teachers."

But her father was very anxious for her to be well educated.

Wherever they went he insisted on finding men, and sometimes women, to teach her subjects he thought she should learn.

Miss Webb had been an exceptional woman, having retired from the position of mistress in a School in Florence.

She wished to visit India, because her brother was in the East India Company.

In six months Zenobia had learnt a great deal from her which she would not have known otherwise.

When she and her father moved on, it had seemed amusing that her next teacher was a very clever Brahmin, who was in need of money.

"At least," she told herself as she went up to her bedroom on returning to Chadwell House, "Papa taught me how to look after myself, and to move quickly."

Lord Chadwell had also taught her to be tactful and intelligent.

She did not wish to arouse her Stepmother's suspicions that she was not accepting what had been arranged for her.

There was a luncheon-party that day in which she was included, and Irene had sent one of her own gowns to wear.

With alterations made by a housemaid, it fitted her.

It was very elaborate and much more expensive than any gown Zenobia had ever possessed.

Later in the afternoon she found a whole pile of her Stepmother's discarded clothes on her bed.

Her first impulse was to throw them back.

She wanted to tell Irene she would not demean herself by wearing anything she had worn.

Her common sense however told her that would be very stupid.

Mr. Williamson had told her what her salary would be, which was considerably more than she had expected.

It was still very little compared to what she and her father had spent during the years they were travelling.

If she was to remain independent and perhaps, when the Earl had finished with her, go abroad, she would need every penny she possessed.

That was, in fact, very little.

She would therefore be extremely foolish to refuse the

beautiful and expensive gowns which she could never afford to buy herself.

With Irene's permission after luncheon she had driven, escorted by the Housekeeper, to visit her father's Solicitors, Burke, Powell, and Burke.

She was received by the senior partner.

He told her frankly that her Stepmother was correct in what she had said.

Her father's money had all been spent, except for about 500 pounds.

This she would have the greatest difficulty in obtaining from the Bank without Lady Chadwell's permission.

The house was mortgaged and the furniture could not be moved or sold without her Guardian's permission, who, of course, was Irene.

"You could fight these matters in the Courts," Mr. Burke told her, "but it would be a long wait and the costs could amount to a large sum of money."

"Thank you, Mr. Burke," Zenobia said. "I just needed to know my position, and I realise there is very little I can do at the moment."

"I think, Miss Chade, you would be well advised to live with your Stepmother, although I expect it will not be long before you leave her to be married."

There was nothing else he could say, Zenobia realised bitterly as she drove away.

When she got back to Chadwell House she could see the triumph in Irene's eyes.

She wanted to tell her what she thought of her.

She longed to denounce her as being everything that was dishonest and unpleasant.

But the years of her father's training stood her in good stead.

With a smile she said:

"You are quite right, Stepmama. Mr. Burke has explained my position and I can only thank you for allowing me to stay here for the moment."

"I thought you would see sense," Irene said, "and I have already asked a man to dinner to-night, who I think would suit you very well."

"How kind of you!" Zenobia murmured, keeping the sarcasm out of her voice.

"His name is Sir Benjamin Fisher," Irene said. "He is half-Jewish, extremely rich, and is looking for an attractive, well-bred wife who will be a help to him socially."

Zenobia said nothing.

When she met Sir Benjamin, she guessed he had been one of her Stepmother's lovers.

He had undoubtedly contributed to the up-keep of the house.

He was, however, nearly fifty, and was very anxious to re-marry.

With a few artless questions Zenobia learnt that he had two daughters by his first marriage, but no son.

Sir Benjamin obviously wished to dazzle her with his riches.

He explained his importance in the City and the brilliant investments he had made in different parts of the Empire.

In fact, he made it very clear that his wife, whoever she was, could, if she wished, wrap herself in sables and festoon herself with diamonds.

"She would look," Zenobia longed to add, "exceedingly vulgar."

She however listened to Sir Benjamin with the look of wide-eyed innocence of a girl who knew nothing of the world.

She knew he was delighted at the idea of becoming her husband.

She went up to bed after an evening of listening to Sir Benjamin.

She had also watched Irene flirting in an outrageous manner with a man who had newly come into her life.

Zenobia washed herself from head to feet in cold water.

She felt unclean at being in the company of anyone who had touched Irene.

*   *   *

Strangely enough, she slept peacefully until her maid called her at six o'clock.

She brought her a cup of tea and a slice of bread and butter.

She said a little doubtfully that breakfast would not be ready before seven o'clock.

"That will be quite soon enough," Zenobia said, "and would you be kind enough to put everything I possess into my trunk?"

"Are you leavin', Miss?" the maid asked. "Her Ladyship didn't say anything about it!"

"I have left a note for Her Ladyship which will explain that I am going away to stay with friends," Zenobia said.

The maid fetched her trunk.

Once again Zenobia thought of her new gowns and felt reluctant to wear anything that had been Irene's.

Then she told herself, "Beggars cannot be choosers."

She said to the housemaid:

"I am taking with me only the trunk with which I arrived and the box of books. If I need them, I will send later for the gowns Her Ladyship had given me, so will you keep them packed up?"

"Of course, Miss," the maid said, "but I'm afraid they'll be very crushed."

"It does not matter," Zenobia said.

A footman came into the room to carry down her trunk.

To his surprise, she asked him to get her a Hackney-carriage.

"I can run round to the stables and tell them you needs one of ours, Miss," he offered.

"Thank you," Zenobia replied, "but I am going only a short way and will be quite all right in a Hackney-carriage."

She handed the note she had written for her Stepmother to the footman and added:

"Will you see that this is placed on Her Ladyship's breakfast-tray?"

Once the trunk and the box of books were packed into the carriage she drove away.

She had left her old life behind and was setting out on what might prove to be a great adventure.

At least she could be her own mistress and be free of Irene, and men like Sir Benjamin Fisher.

"I will fend for myself," she said determinedly, "but at the same time, Papa, you will have to help me."

chapter three

ZENOBIA was fascinated by the Earl's private train which was waiting for them at the platform.

Mr. Williamson was there and informed her she would travel with him in one carriage.

The rest of the staff would be in several others.

The Drawing-Room of which Zenobia caught a glance through the window was very impressive.

Five minutes before the train was due to start, the Earl was carried aboard by several footmen.

His valet was fussing about behind him.

Mr. Williamson was also in attendance.

Zenobia thought with a smile that the Earl certainly saw to his own comfort.

When the train started, Mr. Williamson joined her in the otherwise empty carriage.

As she smiled at him he asked:

"Have you ever been in a private train before?"

"No," Zenobia replied, "and that is one more experience that I can add to many other unusual ones!"

She had the idea that Mr. Williamson was still looking at her with a worried expression in his eyes.

It was as if there were something he wished to say to her.

After a few banal remarks about the weather, she made it easier for him by saying:

"I think you have something to tell me, Mr. Williamson."

"I have been wondering how to phrase it," he replied.

Then after a pause in which they were both silent, he said:

"I feel that I ought to warn you, if you want to keep your position as His Lordship's secretary, not to become too enamoured of him."

Zenobia looked at him in sheer astonishment.

This was something she had certainly not expected, and after a moment she asked:

"Why should you expect that I should?"

"It is something that happens to so many of your sex," Mr. Williamson replied warily. "In fact, His Lordship finds it extremely tiresome that a large number of women in whom he is not the least interested should, to put it frankly, fall in love with him."

Zenobia laughed.

"That is certainly something you need not worry about where I am concerned."

"I hope I can be sure of that."

"Quite sure!" Zenobia asserted. "If ever I am attracted or, as you say, fall in love, it will certainly not be with anybody from the Social World, which I dislike and despise!"

She spoke so violently that Mr. Williamson wondered what had upset her.

He thought it must be a man who had frightened and perhaps distressed her.

He decided therefore it would be a mistake to say any more.

They talked about other things until they were nearly at their destination.

What interested Zenobia was the history of the Castle, which she learned had originally been built in medieval times.

It had however been added to and altered over the centuries until there was practically nothing left of the original building.

Nevertheless, most of the Earl's distinguished ancestors had lived in it.

Mr. Williamson, who was an erudite man, spoke quite interestingly of the many Statesmen and soldiers who had contributed to the fame of the Ockendons.

"I will look for some books to read about them," Zenobia said eagerly. "It will be thrilling to be really living in a place that is part of history, and I am sure His Lordship has a large Library."

"Very large indeed," Mr. Williamson replied, and she smiled with delight.

The journey did not take long.

There were a number of carriages waiting for them at the private Halt which was about three miles from the Castle.

Zenobia learnt from Mr. Williamson there would be a carriage for the Earl, one for them, a brake for the other servants, and another for the luggage.

The Earl's valet, his top Chef, and a young man who Zenobia learned was assistant to Mr. Williamson were all in another.

She was however more interested in the country they

were passing on their way to the Castle than who was in the procession of carriages.

When she had her first glimpse of the Castle, it was exactly as she had hoped it would be.

It was very large, with the centre block having been added in Georgian times.

There were two wings branching out from it, the end of one being all that was left of the medieval Castle.

It shone like a jewel with the trees behind it.

There was a lake in front, and a Park full of very ancient oak trees.

It was just as her father had described an English ancestral house.

Zenobia felt sad that she could never talk to him about it.

He had often told her of the house-parties he had enjoyed when he was a young man.

He had described the Steeple-Chases in which he had taken part.

Also the fêtes and garden-parties that had been attended by everybody of importance.

Zenobia knew that sometimes, although he would not admit it, he missed his own country house in the green of England.

She was sure when they were sweltering in the tropical heat, or thirsty in some desert waste, that his thoughts were on the land he had left behind.

It was also this that made her hate her Stepmother.

She knew that if her mother were alive, they would have been living in the country with their horses and dogs.

By now her father would probably have become the Lord Lieutenant and representative of the Queen.

"It is Irene who has spoilt everything for him!" she had told herself many years ago.

Now she was saying the same thing about herself.

Why could her father not have realised that having married a wife so despicable, she would spend all his money and leave nothing for him when he needed it.

But there was no use looking back to the past.

Zenobia was determined that she would make her own way in the world.

She had been more fortunate than she dared hope in coming to Ockendon Castle.

She thought the Earl was good-looking, obviously intelligent, and she would enjoy working with him.

As for falling in love with him as Mr. Williamson feared, he was quite safe where she was concerned.

What she had heard and seen of London Society disgusted her.

She was sure that the women who pursued the Earl and whom, whatever Mr. Williamson might say, he encouraged, were all like Irene.

They were unfaithful to their husbands and interested only in what they called "love."

Zenobia had a vivid imagination.

She had also seen in India the way a number of ladies whose husbands were sweltering away in the Plains tried to flirt with her father.

They would get her out of the way so that they could do so.

They thought of her as only a child, and children were supposed to have no feelings about the behaviour of grown-ups.

They had no idea how much Zenobia disliked and despised them.

When it was possible, she would put every obstacle in their way.

She would prevent them from being alone with her father.

Some women had even tried to bribe her.

They gave her chocolates and other presents to tell them when her father would be alone.

Also to disappear from his presence when they appeared.

She remembered giving in disgust the chocolates and anything else they offered her to the servants.

She used to persuade her father without very much difficulty that they should move on from where they were staying.

It was not often, in fact, they found themselves in social circles.

Once they had stayed with the Viceroy in Simla, where there were a large number of attractive and unattached wives.

Another time they had been the guests of a Governor of Bombay.

It was just the sort of life, only in a different climate, which Irene would have enjoyed.

Zenobia was deeply prejudiced against it.

She was only eager to return to their travels however primitive and uncomfortable they might be.

Now, she thought, it was very exciting to be at Ockendon Castle.

It was a great relief that as a secretary she would eat alone or perhaps with Mr. Williamson.

She would not be expected to associate with the Earl except in working hours.

The inside of the Castle was even more delightful than she had expected.

Her father had taught her a great deal about art when they lived at one time in Rome.

The moment she saw the pictures she knew she could spend hours looking at them.

She also realised she had a great deal to learn about furniture.

The Library, which was enormous, made her gasp with delight.

There was a Curator, an elderly man with white hair, who she was sure would be able to tell her anything she wanted to know.

She had been given a very pretty bedroom on the first floor, and a young housemaid came to unpack for her.

There was a Sitting-Room next door, where Zenobia thought she would work.

As soon as she arrived, her luncheon was brought there and she was waited on by a footman.

When the maid had unpacked, Zenobia realised there was very little for her to put in the wardrobe.

She almost regretted leaving the expensive and attractive gowns Irene had given her.

She had suddenly felt she could not demean herself by wearing them.

Then she shrugged her shoulders and thought she would certainly not need anything smart in her capacity as secretary.

She was glad she had not obeyed her first idea of being sensible and saving her money.

"I hate Irene!" she said to her reflection in the mirror. "Although it was wonderful for me, she ruined Papa's life, and all those women in the Social World are exactly the same!"

She remembered Sir Benjamin Fisher trying to tempt her with his money.

His promise of diamonds and the fine houses of which she would be chatelaine.

If she had accepted him, as Irene had obviously planned, she would be nothing but a puppet.

Certainly not the real person she wanted to be for the man she married.

She decided that she would never find the right sort of man.

She would therefore be an "Old Maid" for the rest of her life.

"What does it matter?" she asked defiantly. "I can read, and if I can afford it, I can travel as I did with Papa. I will be very much happier that way."

She was feeling in a defiant mood, when a footman knocked on the door.

He told her that His Lordship wished to see her.

The young man guided her along the corridor.

He showed her into what she realised was a Sitting-Room opening out of the Master Bedroom.

It was furnished in a way she would have expected, with deep comfortable leather arm-chairs, and a flat-topped Regency desk.

There were several magnificent pictures by Stubbs on the walls.

The Earl was sitting in a high-backed chair and his injured leg was raised on a stool.

She thought when she entered that he was looking rather pale, as if the journey had been a strain on him.

There was a glass of champagne on one side of him and a number of papers on the other.

"Good-afternoon, Miss Webb!" the Earl said as she approached him. "I hope you have been looked after and are comfortable."

"Yes, thank you, My Lord."

"I thought we might get down to some work," the Earl

said, "and later you should meet my half-sister, Lady Mary, who lives in the East Wing."

Zenobia was surprised. Nobody had mentioned Lady Mary until now.

"Your half-sister?" she asked involuntarily.

"She is very much older than I am, since my father was first married when he was very young, and his wife died in childbirth," the Earl explained. "I thought you would wish to know that as Lady Mary lives in the house, you are conventionally chaperoned."

Zenobia smiled.

"It is something I never thought about."

"It had not occurred to me, as I was not expecting to have a female secretary," the Earl said, "but when I informed Lady Mary of my arrival, I also told her that you would be staying in the Castle."

Zenobia did not speak and he went on:

"Later, of course, I shall be giving parties, but I was thinking just now when I was having luncheon alone that until some friends of mine arrive, it might speed up the task in front of us if we ate together."

He spoke in a dry, disinterested voice.

It convinced Zenobia he was simply thinking of the Exhibition.

He obviously had no other reason for desiring her company.

"I will do exactly as you wish, My Lord," she said, "and I am sure, as you have already said, if the Exhibition is to be a success, the sooner you get in touch with those who you hope will be bringing or sending Exhibits from abroad, the better!"

"I have already worked out this list for India," the Earl said.

He handed her a sheet of paper.

Zenobia sat down and read what he had given her.

It was a list of Princes and Maharajahs, together with one or more possession of each of them which he thought would be of interest to the British public.

Zenobia thought that most of the items were an excellent choice.

At the same time, there were not, she thought, enough of them.

Considering how important India had become to the Empire, there should be many more.

A little tentatively she said:

"I see Your Lordship has not included the Rajput pictures belonging to the Maharata of Udaipur. As I think they are the best collection in India, you must try to persuade him to lend some of them for the Exhibition."

The Earl stared at her before he asked:

"Are you telling me you have seen the pictures?"

"Yes, My Lord."

Zenobia did not add that she and her father had stayed with the Maharata in his Palace.

She thought Udaipur was one of the loveliest places she had ever seen.

"You surprise me, Miss Webb!" the Earl said. "As I have not had the privilege, as you have, of seeing these pictures, perhaps you could make it clear to His Highness which ones we particularly want."

"I will do that, My Lord," Zenobia agreed.

"Have you any other suggestions?"

It was obvious that he thought it unlikely and was still suspicious that in some way she was deceiving him.

"The jewels of the Nizam of Hyderabad are very famous!"

"Good heavens! Have I left him off the list?" the Earl asked.

Zenobia handed him back the piece of paper he had given her and he said:

"An oversight on my part. I stayed at the Residency in Hyderabad, and I certainly meant to include his jewels. As I expect you know, the Kohinoor was found in one of the Nizam's own mines."

Zenobia smiled, but she did not reply, and after a moment the Earl asked:

"How is it possible that at your age you should know so much about India and have visited parts where I have never been?"

"My employer was a great traveller, My Lord."

"So it seems!" the Earl answered. "And where else in the world are you suggesting we go for treasures?"

Zenobia had already thought this out.

She gave him a list which included some of the treasures of Ceylon.

There was also an outstanding statue of Buddha in Burma, and another from North Borneo.

She did not notice the surprise in the Earl's eyes as she went on:

"I did not have the privilege of seeing the earlier Exhibitions, although I have read about them. It seems to me that many places on the route to the Orient were not represented."

The Earl did not speak and she continued:

"For instance, Gibraltar, Malta, Singapore, and Hong Kong. Surely there are treasures there which no one has seen before, and perhaps also in St. Helena, where Napoleon died."

She smiled as she added:

"Or the Ascension Islands, where the Lord Mayor of London's turtles come from?"

Still unaware that the Earl was almost gaping at her, she continued:

"There are places too like the Spice Islands, the Solomons and the Leewards, which must surely have one or two things worth showing, and there are other islands which never have any attention, but which would be thrilled if you approached them."

She paused before she added:

"I am thinking of the Chagos Islands, the Diamond Rock, which is very small, but was garrisoned by the Navy in the Napoleonic Wars, and given the prefix 'H.M.S.'"

She drew in her breath and the Earl ejaculated:

"How in the name of Heaven can you know all this? And do not tell me you have visited all these places, for I will not believe you!"

"Certainly not all of them," Zenobia replied, "but I have visited many others, which I think are worth your attention. You will doubtless remember Cyprus, for which the British pay 92,800 pounds a year in tribute to the Sublime Porte, together with four million okes of salt."

"I think I am dreaming!" the Earl said. "At any moment I will wake up to find you are not there!"

Zenobia laughed.

It was a very natural, pretty, and unaffected sound.

"I am only trying to help Your Lordship."

"You are certainly surprising me," he replied, "and before we go any further, I would like to know a great deal more about you than I know at the moment."

Zenobia stiffened and looked away from him.

Then as he waited she said:

"I am sure Your Lordship realises that a good secretary should be impersonal."

"Are you rebuking me?" the Earl enquired.

"I should not presume to do anything so . . .

impertinent," Zenobia answered, "but I have no wish to talk about . . . myself, but only about the . . . Exhibition."

There was a defiance in her voice which the Earl did not miss.

As if he thought it would be a mistake to press her, he merely said:

"Very well, Miss Webb, we will return to our work, and perhaps you will tell me who else you wish to include on your list."

In what she thought was a crisp, businesslike manner, but which actually was soft and musical, Zenobia replied:

"I see, of course, Your Lordship has written down Australia and New Zealand, Canada and South Africa, but there are also British settlers on the Falklands, and the sugar islands of the Caribbean, Bermuda, and Fiji."

"Those shall be included, if we have the time," the Earl remarked, "although I doubt if some of them could produce anything worth showing."

He spoke as if he were trying to score off her for being too clever.

As she was aware of it, Zenobia could not help saying:

"There is a tribe in the desert south of Algiers who carve the most strange and fantastic images of themselves, rather in the same way that the negroes do in Haiti."

"I can see you are a mine of information, Miss Webb!" the Earl remarked.

Somehow he did not make it sound a compliment.

At the end of an hour they had a very long list of potential Exhibitors.

Zenobia was sure if they wrote to them all and had a good response, there would be enough material to fill the Albert Hall half-a-dozen times.

Therefore, having shown the Earl that she could be indispensable to him, she began to cut down.

She chose those who were most likely to provide something sensational.

They would, she suggested, leave the less important to fill in the gaps where they received a refusal.

She was so interested in what they were talking about and what they were deciding.

She had no idea what the Earl was thinking.

He thought that as she scribbled away on a piece of paper with which he had provided her she looked ridiculously young.

She was also so lovely that it was impossible to believe she could be so intelligent.

He found the dark blue of her eyes intriguing, while her eye-lashes curled upwards like those of a child.

They were a deeper gold than her hair, which seemed to have touches of silver in it.

Her gown was plain, but it revealed the curves of her figure.

Every movement she made was graceful, almost as if she had been trained as a dancer.

The idea kept occurring to the Earl that she must be putting on an act.

She could not possibly be as genuine as she sounded.

Yet, when he tested her about the countries he knew and had visited himself, her replies were always correct.

She did not hesitate to admit ignorance if she did not know the answer.

He thought that if she had been pretending to be clever, she would not have been so frank.

"She is certainly a secretary I never expected to find," the Earl told himself.

Their list was finished, at least for the moment, and Zenobia said:

"If Your Lordship wishes, I will start immediately to

write the letters, starting with India. Obviously their exhibits will be larger and much more important than anybody else's."

"You have a Sitting-Room next to your bedroom," the Earl replied, "and if there is anything you need, just ask Mr. Williamson."

"Thank you, My Lord."

Zenobia got to her feet.

Then she hesitated before she asked:

"Have I Your Lordship's permission to approach your Curator when I have any free time? I am very anxious to see more of the Castle and, if it is permitted, to borrow books from the Library."

"That request does not surprise me," the Earl smiled, "and you certainly have my permission to read every book the Library contains, if you are here long enough. I expect you will also enjoy seeing the grounds and the stables."

There was a light in Zenobia's eyes.

As if he read her thoughts, the Earl added:

"I suppose, seeing how much you have travelled, you are fond of riding."

Zenobia gave a little cry of joy.

"Is Your Lordship saying I might be allowed to ride your horses?"

"I think it would be very ungracious if I refused, but unfortunately I cannot supply you with a yak or a reluctant mule!"

Zenobia laughed.

"I might prefer a camel, but will be very content with a spirited horse!"

"You must tell my grooms what you require," the Earl said, "and I do not think you will be disappointed."

Zenobia was just beginning to thank him, when the door opened and a woman came in.

Zenobia guessed before the Earl spoke that this must be Lady Mary.

She was aware that the newcomer gave her a hard, scrutinising look as she advanced towards the Earl's chair.

She was a tall woman, middle-aged, with hair that was beginning to turn grey at the temples.

'She might have been good-looking when she was young,' Zenobia thought, 'perhaps even pretty.'

Now her skin was sallow and there were lines under her eyes and at the sides of her mouth.

She was dressed in a rather unbecoming tweed skirt and jacket.

She wore flat shoes that seemed to make her move purposefully in an almost masculine manner.

She reached the Earl's chair.

Sharply, in a voice that was deeper than that of the average woman, she said:

"I cannot imagine why I am never told you intend visiting us before you are actually in the house, D'Arcy!"

"The doctors only decided late on Tuesday evening that I was well enough to leave London, and as I was bored with them and felt I could get stronger in the fresh air, I came home immediately!"

"Well, you are here now," Lady Mary said, "and I hope I shall see something of you."

"I hope so, too," the Earl replied lightly, "but actually I am here to work."

"To work?" Lady Mary enquired with an incredulous note in her voice.

Now she looked directly at Zenobia.

"Let me introduce Miss Webb," the Earl said, "who is helping me as my secretary to arrange an Exhibition which is taking place next year at the Royal Albert Hall."

"Are you saying this is your—*secretary?*" Lady Mary asked.

Her voice insinuated something very different.

"It seems hard to credit, when she appears so young, but Miss Webb has travelled a great deal and actually speaks *Urdu, Tamil,* and many other Eastern languages, besides being proficient in European ones."

As he said her name, Zenobia dropped Lady Mary a small curtsy.

The older woman did not put out her hand.

She merely looked her up and down.

Zenobia thought it was a somewhat insulting fashion. Then Lady Mary said:

"You always have very plausible excuses for anything you do, D'Arcy, but an Exhibition is certainly an original one!"

"It is the Queen's idea," the Earl replied, quite unperturbed. "It is the Colonial and Indian Exhibition which is to take place at the Royal Albert Hall in May, and is to be as good as the famous one arranged by the Prince Consort, when he was alive, at the Crystal Palace."

"I should think that is impossible!" Lady Mary retorted.

"I am inclined to agree with you," the Earl answered, "but at least I shall have done my best. If you are interested, Miss Webb can show you the list we have already compiled of possible Exhibitors who live in every part of the globe which is painted red on the map!"

Lady Mary was not amused at what the Earl intended to be a joke.

Instead, she said:

"When you have time to see me *alone,* D'Arcy, I have a number of complaints to make about the way things are run on the Estate and in the house, and I think you will be wise to listen to me."

"I will certainly do that, Mary, as soon as I have time," the Earl replied.

"I am sure Miss Webb will keep you *very* busy!" Lady Mary answered.

There was a perceptible pause before the last word.

As she walked towards the door, Zenobia knew from the expression on her face that she was suspicious of what was her true position in her brother's life.

She was also extremely antagonistic.

As the door shut behind her, the Earl gave a sigh.

"I am sorry if my sister seemed rude," he said, "but she is always very difficult with all my friends, and makes continual complaints about the staff, which, naturally, they resent."

"And yet you let her live here!" Zenobia said without thinking. "That is kind of you."

As she spoke she thought perhaps it was impertinent to say anything so intimate.

"She, of course, lived here when my father was alive," the Earl replied, "and when I inherited I felt it ungracious to turn her out, especially as the house is so big. Then when I offered her the Dower House, which is very attractive, she refused to leave."

He spoke almost as if he were talking to himself.

Then, as if thinking it was a mistake, he said sharply:

"I am sure you want to get on with your work, Miss Webb, and I will be thinking of what particular Exhibits we should ask for in the next country we write to after you have finished with India."

"Very good, My Lord, and I will bring you the letters as soon as they are finished," Zenobia replied.

She went to the door.

When she reached it she remembered she should curtsy, and looked back.

She was then aware that the Earl was watching her.

She wondered if he was still unconvinced that she was not deceiving him in some way.

She suddenly felt shy and hurried from the room.

She went down the passage, then up the stairs to her own Sitting-Room.

The maid, whose name, she had heard, was Lucy, had unpacked for her.

As she came into the room she put the papers down on a table near the window.

"I thought I 'eard you, Miss," Lucy said. "Would you like a cup of tea?"

"I would love one!" Zenobia answered. "Thank you for thinking of it."

"I'm 'ere to look after you, Miss, and just you ask me if there's anythin' you want."

"I will do that," Zenobia replied.

"We finds it rather dull here when there's no one staying in the Castle and 'Is Lordship, being so ill, has been away a long time."

"Does he ordinarily have big parties?" Zenobia asked.

"Sometimes," Lucy answered, "but usually it's half-a-dozen of 'is special friends, but none of the lovely ladies in whom 'Is Lordship's interested, as you might say."

Zenobia knew exactly what Lucy meant and her lips tightened.

"It's because 'e's so 'andsome!" the maid went on. "They all falls in love with 'im an' breaks their 'earts. It's sad sometimes."

"I am sure it must be," Zenobia replied in a tight little voice.

"Wot my mother always said was: 'Men are men, an' there's nothin' you can do about it!' But 'Is Lordship's exceptional, an' we're all very proud of 'im."

"Proud of him? Why?"

"Oh, it's not just 'cause 'e's good-looking, Miss, it's not only that," Lucy said. "It's 'cause he got two medals for gallantry when he was in the Army. He saved a boy's life here, when 'e fell in the lake and couldn't swim, and there's no one can ride an 'orse like 'Is Lordship can!"

Zenobia, however, was not convinced.

She was sure the Earl was just like the other men who had hung around her Stepmother until her father had left her.

Then there was the Prince of Wales, who, if gossip was to be believed, was unfaithful to the beautiful Princess Alexandra with every woman who went to Marlborough House.

Zenobia's father had never been interested in gossip.

But it had been impossible not to be aware that people were talking about the Prince of Wales in every country they visited.

Lord Chadwell was an important man.

Immediately on his arrival in any Capital City he always received an invitation to the British Embassy.

He felt it only polite to accept.

He had taken Zenobia with him, even when she was small.

She had found the conversation invariably got round to the Royal Family.

While they praised the Queen, although they deprecated her long period of mourning, there was an undoubted excitement in their voices when they discussed the Prince of Wales.

They drooled over the latest Beauty who was always at his side.

They had little social life in Devonshire.

Yet those who did call on them invariably spoke of the "Marlborough House Set."

After murmuring conventionally how much they admired the Princess of Wales, their voices would drop almost to a whisper as they added:

"Of course, we are sorry for her! Poor dear! How she must suffer, but she never reveals her feelings in public."

Zenobia did not join in, but she would listen.

She thought that the Prince should not set such a bad example.

He should behave with the same dignity and pride her father had always shown.

"That sort of society need never worry him again!" she told herself.

The same applied to herself.

But here she was, when she least expected it, working for a member of the Social World.

His morals were, she was sure, no better than Irene's.

As far as she was concerned, they were two of a kind.

chapter four

ZENOBIA worked in her Sitting-Room.

She was surprised when Lucy came to tell her that a bath was ready for her in her bedroom. She had no idea it was so late.

Almost reluctantly she put the pages aside.

She knew as she did so she had enjoyed writing the letters.

Some of them to people she knew and others to those she had heard of when she was in India.

She was thinking about India all the time she was bathing.

Lucy helped her into one of her only two evening-gowns.

She wondered if she was smart enough to dine with the Earl.

The gowns she had worn in Devonshire with her father were very simple.

At the same time, although she did not realise it, they made her look very attractive.

They suited her far better than the elaborate, over-decorated gown which Irene had lent her the night she had been in London.

She looked at herself in the mirror.

She wondered whether, if there were any other people present, the Earl would be ashamed of her.

Then she felt that was not a question she should be asking as a secretary.

"All he should be concerned with is my brain!" she said mockingly.

She turned away from the mirror, uninterested in her own appearance.

She found the Earl waiting for her in what was known as the Silver Salon.

Then she did feel inadequate beside his magnificence.

He had changed into evening-clothes.

A wheel-chair had been produced so that he could be pushed into the Dining-Room.

Even so, it was impossible not to admire his square shoulders and the way his evening-coat fitted without a wrinkle.

She thought that his stiff white shirt made him look somehow different and more masculine than he had in the daytime.

"You are punctual, Miss Webb," the Earl said when she appeared, "which is unusual in a woman."

"But very necessary in a secretary," Zenobia retorted.

He smiled at the swiftness with which she replied.

He offered her a glass of champagne, which she refused.

One of the footmen wheeled him into the Dining-Room with Zenobia walking beside him.

As she expected, the Dining-Room was very impressive with portraits of Ockendons in elaborate gold frames decorating the walls.

An extremely fine marble mantelpiece had been carved by a famous Italian sculptor.

The food was delicious and they were waited on by two footmen and the Butler.

Zenobia found that she and the Earl had so much to discuss about the Exhibition.

In fact, she hardly had time to appreciate the excellence of the food.

He insisted she should have a glass of wine.

"Food and wine go together!" he said firmly. "You will doubtless tell me that tradition goes back to Olympus."

"I wondered if Your Lordship would remember what you enjoyed when you were one with the gods!" Zenobia said mischievously.

The Earl laughed.

She had spoken as she would have to her father.

She had forgotten for the moment that she should be quiet and subservient.

When she quickly returned to their discussion of the Exhibition, the Earl said:

"Now that the servants have left the room, I can ask you again to tell me about yourself. You must be aware that I am extremely curious, for you are certainly a very unusual secretary."

Zenobia thought for a moment. Then she said:

"Perhaps I am wise to leave you curious, so that you will not get bored with me, which, I understand, is a habit of yours where people are concerned."

She hoped she was not being impertinent, and the Earl asked:

"Who has been talking to you?"

"Can you expect the people who know you to do anything else?" Zenobia asked.

"What I am really wondering," the Earl replied, "is why

you are not enjoying yourself in London, as you should be, attending Balls, and being followed around by an admiring throng of young men."

He spoke half-mockingly and half-seriously and Zenobia answered:

"That, to me, is a way of life I hate and despise! Nothing could make me accept it."

"You are implying," the Earl protested, "that it is what you could be doing, and what, if you are truthful, is yours by right."

He was too perceptive, she thought.

What he said made her remember it was exactly what Irene had intended in order to be quickly rid of her.

"I dislike London Society and everybody in it!" she said. "I consider that what you have just described as being almost compulsory for the majority of young women is an intolerable imposition, in which they lose not only their freedom but also their self-respect."

"Now, why should you think that?" the Earl argued. "Where unmarried ladies are concerned, where else are they to meet their future husbands?"

"Only, as you are suggesting, in the marriage market, which is utterly degrading and something to which I would never submit!"

She spoke defiantly, then added angrily:

"Gentlemen may think they can buy a wife as they would buy a horse, and that both should be grateful to them, but as far as I am concerned, it is something I would never tolerate, so I will never marry!"

She spoke positively and the Earl, sitting back in his chair, said:

"That is the one foolish thing you have said since we met. Of course you must marry! Do you really intend to spend the rest of your life pretending to be a superior servant rather than have a husband who will give you every luxury and, because you are so good-looking, will undoubtedly fall genuinely in love with you."

"There is a question-mark where that is concerned," Zenobia answered. "When a woman is married, it is far more likely that her husband will be pursuing some other female whose face he finds more attractive than hers!"

She spoke so scathingly that the Earl laughed.

"I suppose," he said after a moment, "you are so young that you have not yet fallen in love. When you do, you will find it is up to you to keep your husband captive and not let him go a-roaming."

"As I do not intend to marry," Zenobia said coldly, "I shall be unable to prove Your Lordship wrong. Now let us talk about something more interesting."

"I find you extremely interesting, Miss Webb," the Earl replied, "and if I really thought you were speaking the truth in saying you will never marry, I should be extremely perturbed."

"Why?" Zenobia asked.

"Because it is unnatural. Every woman needs a husband, and it must be the ambition of every young girl who is born into the Social World to find one as quickly as possible. Otherwise she will find herself and 'Old Maid.'"

"I was thinking only to-day," Zenobia answered, "that that is what I will be. If I have enough money to travel, then I should be completely content to live a life that I would really enjoy."

"Alone?" the Earl asked.

"I have never had any difficulty in making friends with the natives of any country in which I have lived. I find them much more fascinating than the English or French aristocrats, who are far too puffed up with their own consequence!"

She paused for a moment before she went on:

"I made friends with a woman in Sarawak whose husband was a head-hunter, and I enjoyed her company in the same way as I enjoyed talking with the Berber women in Africa."

"Every woman, if she is normal," the Earl said, "needs men, not women in her life."

"Of course I enjoy being with men," Zenobia said. "I find some of them extremely interesting, but I have no wish to marry a Bedouin Chief or even a Sultan who already has four wives and a large number of other women in his Harem!"

"You are trying to twist what I am saying, and avoid giving me a straight answer," the Earl complained. "What I would like to know is why you have such a hatred of marriage. Has somebody you loved deserted you?"

"No, of course not!" Zenobia replied.

"Then what has forced you into celibacy?"

"That is a secret, My Lord, and it is something I have no wish to talk about."

"I have never met a more infuriating young woman!" the Earl said sharply. "You know perfectly well it is bad for me, when I have been so ill, to be frustrated and not allowed to have my own way!"

Zenobia laughed, then she said:

"That shows you have been spoilt since childhood. I am sure it is good for you to realise there is one person, even if it is only an insignificant one, who will not give in to your every whim."

"That is a challenge, Miss Webb!"

*   *   *

Zenobia went to bed almost as soon as they left the Dining-Room, not only because she was tired.

She knew it would be a mistake for the Earl to stay up late after being so ill.

When she was in the dark she thought over what had been said after the servants left the Dining-Room.

She decided it was an extremely strange conversation to have with her employer.

At the same time, she had enjoyed it.

If she was truthful, she had been happy for the first time since her father's death.

It had been very lonely in their house in Devonshire when the Funeral was over.

She had been apprehensive all the way on the journey to London about meeting Irene.

After meeting her, she had been scared because she had no money and feared she would really have to live with her Stepmother.

She feared, too, finding herself married by compulsion to somebody like Sir Benjamin and then being unable to escape.

Now, unless she was very unfortunate, Irene would have no idea where she was.

She thought, because her Stepmother was interested in no one but herself, she would not try very hard to find her.

"I must not offend or upset the Earl," she admonished herself.

At the same time, she had no intention of gratifying his curiosity.

She did not wish to tell him anything more than was necessary as to why she was earning her own living.

She was surprised that he considered it important that she should be chaperoned.

She thought a little wryly that Lady Mary would certainly not be particularly kind or pleasant in that position.

As she fell asleep she was saying a prayer of thankfulness that she had been able to get away.

To have found what she knew would be an absorbing task in helping the Earl with the Exhibition.

When she awoke she began to think of more people they could approach and other treasures she and her father had seen on their journeys.

Then she found it was only six o'clock in the morning.

She remembered that the Earl had said she could ride his horses.

Dressing herself in a habit in which she had ridden with her father in Devonshire, she went to the stables.

She asked if they would saddle her a horse.

She knew the grooms were surprised to see her so early.

She explained that she had His Lordship's permission.

Refusing the offer that a groom should ride with her, she set off alone.

She guessed there would be somewhere where she could gallop safely without there being too many rabbit-holes.

She found some level ground at the far end of the Park after she had passed through a wood to reach it.

She galloped until both she and the horse felt their blood throbbing with the excitement of it.

Then reluctantly she returned home.

She told herself that she must have breakfast and be ready soon after nine o'clock in case the Earl sent for her.

She had, however, no intention of wasting her time.

Once she had changed from her riding-habit into a simple morning gown, she had breakfast.

Then she sat down at her desk.

She started to write more letters to India.

She was careful to get the titles of the ruling Princes right, and add their decorations after their names.

She decided, however, that she should check these to make sure she had made no mistake.

After she had written three letters she went to find the Curator of the Library.

He had a small office a long way down the passage.

When she introduced herself, he said he was sure he could find out what she wanted.

Otherwise he would get in touch immediately with the India Office.

She thanked him.

While he was looking through his catalogue she went into the Library.

It was as if she were drawn to it irresistibly.

She wandered round, staring up at the shelves.

She was thinking it was difficult to decide which books to read first.

She was determined to read as many as possible while she was at the Castle.

Then she heard somebody come into the Library behind her.

She thought it was the Curator, and asked:

"Have you had any luck?"

When she turned round, she saw it was Lady Mary.

She was looking even more austere than she had the previous day.

To Zenobia's surprise, she walked towards her and said quite pleasantly:

"Good-morning, Miss Webb! I thought you would be impressed by the Library and the number of books we possess!"

"I am indeed!" Zenobia replied. "And I am hoping I shall be able to read a large number of them."

"If you are here!"

Then, lowering her voice, Lady Mary went on:

"That is something I wish to speak to you about. Come to the window, where we cannot be overheard."

Zenobia thought it was very strange.

She followed Lady Mary to one of the large diamond-paned windows which looked out over the garden.

There was a padded window-seat on which they could both sit down.

As they did so, Lady Mary said, still in a lowered tone:

"You may think it strange, but if you are wise, you will leave here as soon as possible!"

There was a pause before Zenobia asked:

"Why should I do that?"

"I am speaking for your own good," Lady Mary replied. "You have made a very grave mistake in taking up a position with His Lordship, and one you may bitterly regret!"

Zenobia thought that Lady Mary was warning her, as Mr. Williamson had done, against falling in love with the Earl.

She wondered how she could tell her she was not interested in her half-brother as a a man without it sounding very rude.

"What you do not know," Lady Mary was saying, "and I suspect no one else will tell you, is that the Earl is a murderer!"

Zenobia stiffened.

Then she gave a little gasp.

"A murderer?" she repeated.

Lady Mary nodded her head.

"Everybody here is forbidden to speak about it. But he murdered his wife by pushing her out of an upstairs window after they had had a series of quarrels which ended in his losing his temper."

"I can hardly believe that!" Zenobia said. "And I did not know he had been married."

"Everybody keeps very quiet about it," Lady Mary said, "but as you bear a faint resemblance to the poor girl who was his wife for only six months, I am telling you, if you value your life, to leave quickly!"

Zenobia stared at her.

She felt that what she was hearing could not be true.

Yet the way Lady Mary spoke seemed very convincing.

"But surely," she said aloud, "if His Lordship really did anything so terrible as to commit murder, he would have been brought to trail and hanged."

"He would have been," Lady Mary answered, "but he was saved before he could be brought before the Justices by two people who lied in his defence."

She gave a deep sigh.

"It was all very upsetting at the time, amd most people have forgotten. But when I saw you, so young, so trusting, and with, as I say, a resemblance to his poor wife, I knew I must tell you the truth!"

It sounded very plausible.

But Zenobia felt instinctively there was something behind Lady Mary's apparent concern for her.

It was not because she really cared for her safety.

Her unusual faculty of perception, which she had always used in dealing with the strange people she met with her father, told her that Lady Mary had no wish for her to be here in the Castle.

At the same time, what she had said seemed incredible.

How could she invent such a fantastic story against her own kin?

"How long ago did this happen?" Zenobia asked.

Before Lady Mary could reply, the Curator, whose name was Mr. Hedges, came into the Library.

He had his catalogue in his hand.

He came towards Zenobia as he started to say:

"I have found what you want, Miss We—"

Then when he saw Lady Mary, his manner changed. In a very different voice he said:

"Good-morning, My Lady!"

"Good-morning, Mr. Hedges! I hope you are trying to put the books into better order than they are at present. It took me nearly an hour last week to find the one I wanted."

"I am sorry about that, My Lady," Mr. Hedges said apologetically, "and if you had asked me, I would have found it for you."

"I like to do things for myself!" Lady Mary snapped. "I intend to speak to His Lordship about your indolence during his absence, and see if he can get better attention than I do regarding the things that need to be done!"

She left the window-seat as she spoke.

She had already walked a little way towards the door before, as if having forgotten her very existence, she suddenly remembered Zenobia.

She turned round to say:

"Remember what I have told you, Miss Webb!"

"Yes, of course, My Lady, and thank you very much," Zenobia replied.

Mr. Hedges did not speak until he was sure Lady Mary was out of earshot.

Then he said, as if he were talking to himself:

"Complaints, always complaints! Never satisfied! This would be a happy place otherwise."

Then as if he felt he had been indiscreet, he said quickly:

"I have found what you want, Miss Webb, and will get it for you at once."

"It is *An Historical Sketch of the Native States of India in Subsidiary Alliances with the British Government,* written by Colonel G. D. Malleson," Mr. Hedges replied.

"That sounds exactly what I need," Zenobia smiled.

Mr. Hedges hurried round the shelves to find the book for which he was looking.

Zenobia wondered almost frantically if what Lady Mary had told her was true.

How could it be possible that the Earl, who was so magnificent and so intelligent, could have done anything so terrible as to murder his wife?

It could only be an exaggeration.

Perhaps even a complete invention on the part of his half-sister.

And yet the way Lady Mary had spoken had been very convincing.

At the same time, distinctly frightening.

'She was not thinking of my interest, that is obvious!' Zenobia thought. 'At the same time, could she really invent such a ridiculous story if there was not some truth in it?'

Then she realised how she could find out whether or not the Earl had been married.

Slowly she walked to where Mr. Hedges had climbed up the moving step-ladder.

He was taking down a book from a shelf that nearly touched the ceiling.

She looked up at him and he said:

"Here it is, Miss Webb."

"Thank you, that is just what I need," Zenobia said, "and where are the other reference books?"

"On the third shelf from the bottom, Miss Webb."

As Mr. Hedges started to climb down the ladder, Zenobia saw what she wanted.

It was the most recent edition of *Debrett's Peerage*.

She took it from the shelf.

When Mr. Hedges handed her the book he was carrying, she said:

"This will be very helpful in what I am doing for His Lordship. I should be grateful if you could also find out whether you have any books describing the treasures of India, Ceylon, the Malay Federated States, and Labuan."

"I will certainly look for them," Mr. Hedges replied, "and I understand this all concerns the Exhibition next year."

"That is right," Zenobia smiled, "and I am sure I shall be asking you for a great deal of help."

"It will be a pleasure, Miss Webb."

Because she was so anxious to know if Lady Mary had spoken the truth, Zenobia hurried up the stairs to her Sitting-Room.

She opened the copy of *Debrett* on a table in the window.

It was easy to find Ockendon in the *Peerage*.

There were not a large number of entries under "O". The Ockendon family filled a page and a half.

Zenobia's eyes were only on the first entry.

This told her that the present and ninth Earl of Ockendon had been married eleven years ago to Briget Patricia Jane, daughter of the Duke of Dorset.

She had died six months after their marriage.

So it was true!

Even so, Zenobia stared at the words as if she found the whole entry as incredible as Lady Mary's story.

She did not know why it surprised her so much.

But everybody had spoken as if the Earl were a bachelor.

Mr. Williamson had said he had no wish to be married, but he had not added the very significant word "again."

It was certainly very strange.

At the same time, it made Zenobia feel uncomfortable that Lady Mary should wish her to leave.

Also, if she were honest, that she was in the company of a murderer.

She had met murderers on her travels with her father— of course she had!

The Chiefs they had met in Sarawak boasted of the heads some of them wore at their waists, or which hung up outside the huts in which they lived.

There had been Maharajahs in India who were known to have captured and tortured to death their enemies.

Sheiks in Africa spoke with pride of the numbers of other tribes they had exterminated in one way or another.

In England, however, it was different.

The Earl, whatever else he might be, was a gentleman, as her father had been.

How could she believe he would deliberately take the life of his bride because he had lost his temper.

Zenobia wondered what he would say if she confronted him with the story.

Then, because she felt far too shy to do so, she decided she would ask Mr. Williamson.

As there was no message from the Earl requesting her presence, she went downstairs to the hall.

She asked a footman to take her to the office where she could find Mr. Williamson.

She was shown down the passage that led towards the Dining-Room.

The footman opened a door before they reached it.

Zenobia found herself in a very large Estate Office with maps on the walls.

A number of tin boxes lay on the table, all inscribed with the Earl's name and his coronet.

Mr. Williamson and his assistant were busy at their desks.

They both rose when Zenobia was shown in.

It was obvious that Mr. Williamson was pleased to see her.

"Good-morning, Miss Webb!" he said. "This is a pleasant surprise, and I hope I can assist you, if that is why you have come here to see me."

"You are quite right, Mr. Williamson," Zenobia said, "but could I talk to you alone?"

Mr. Williamson looked in the direction of his assistant, who immediately left the room.

As the door shut behind him, Zenobia sat down on the opposite side of the desk to Mr. Williamson.

As he also seated himself, he said:

"I hope you have found everything you wanted, and I am sure you are enjoying the Castle."

"It is wonderful!" Zenobia replied. "And as His Lordship allowed me to ride this morning, I am very happy and very grateful to be here."

"That is what I wanted to hear!" Mr. Williamson said with satisfaction.

Zenobia drew in her breath. Then she said:

"However . . . something has just happened that has . . . upset me."

Mr. Williamson gave her a sharp glance.

She knew he was thinking that it concerned the Earl.

"There is nobody else I can talk to about it except you," Zenobia said, "and I only hope you will not feel I am being indiscreet in mentioning it at all."

"You can tell me anything you wish, Miss Webb," Mr. Williamson said, "and you must be aware that I am only too willing to be of help."

Because she felt it embarrassing, Zenobia did not look at him.

She related in a quiet voice what Lady Mary had said.

Mr. Williamson gave a deep sigh as Zenobia finished by asking:

"It seems incredible, but is there any truth in it?"

There was an obvious pause before Mr. Williamson, with what Zenobia thought was an effort, said:

"I will tell you what happened, Miss Webb, but I can only regret that Lady Mary has taken it upon herself to speak about something we were all instructed at the time by His Lordship's father, the Eighth Earl, never to reveal to anyone!"

Zenobia stared at him. Then she asked:

"Are you telling me it is true?"

"It is certainly not true that His Lordship murdered his wife," Mr. Williamson replied, "and it is very wrong and disgraceful of Lady Mary to say such a thing!"

"Then . . . what did happen?" Zenobia enquired.

Mr. Williamson drew in a deep breath before he began:

"When His Lordship, who, of course, was the Viscount in those days, was at Oxford, he and a number of his, shall I say, more spirited friends, all young aristocrats, were given a lecture by some visiting Professor."

He saw Zenobia was listening intently and went on:

"He expressed the opinion that no young man of their age was capable of deciding his own life, not only as regards the profession in which they might excel, but also when it came to marriage, of choosing the right wife who would be a responsible mother for their children."

Mr. Williamson's voice was scathing as he continued:

"It was a most idiotic lecture and bound to make those who listened to it feel rebellious and determined to prove the speaker wrong."

Zenobia smiled.

"I can understand that."

"What happened was inevitable," Mr. Williamson said.

"The more spirited of the students, of which His Lordship was one, decided after a very riotous dinner at which they had all drunk too much, that they would all get married!"

"Married!" Zenobia exclaimed.

"Unfortunately, near Oxford at the time," Mr. Williamson continued, "there was one of those Chapels which no longer exist, in which, because they were private yet consecrated, the incumbent could perform marriages without a licence and without banns, as is compulsory in other Churches."

"I have read about them." Zenobia murmured.

Mr. Williamson went on:

"Ten of the young men who naturally enough had girlfriends with whom they dined and danced when they were not pursuing their studies, picked up the object of their affection and set out for the Chapel in the middle of the night."

Zenobia drew in her breath.

"They woke up the incumbent," Mr. Williamson went on, "and most irresponsibly, in fact disgracefully, he married them!"

"It does not seem . . . possible!" Zenobia murmured.

"That is what his late Lordship said when he heard about it," Mr. Williamson replied. "I had only just begun to work for him in those days, and I knew how shocked and distressed he was, and so was Lady Mary."

There was a pause.

Then as if he were looking back, he said:

"There was, however, where His present Lordship was concerned, a mitigating circumstance."

"What was that?"

"The girl he married was not, as you might say, one of the Oxford girls like those his friends married, but the daughter of the Duke of Dorset."

Zenobia knew that was what she had read in *Debrett*, but she did not speak.

Mr. Williamson continued:

"Lady Briget was staying at an Hotel because she was visiting her brother who was also up at Christ Church with His Lordship. She was an extremely pretty young woman, and I think His Lordship, having met her two or three times, was already attracted to her. Anyway, she obviously was enamoured of him."

Remembering what Mr. Williamson had said previously, Zenobia thought this was understandable.

Her eyes were fixed on his face as he went on:

"I do not know, but perhaps the Duke was already envisaging that a marriage between his daughter and the son of the Earl of Ockendon could prove a very satisfactory alliance.

"There seems to be no other explanation as to why Lady Briget should have consented to be married in such a peculiar fashion in the middle of the night."

"But the marriage was legal?" Zenobia questioned.

"Several of the young men's fathers contested the ceremony on the grounds that their sons were not of age, and as their natural Guardians they had not given their consent to the marriage, so that it was therefore null and void."

"And they succeeded?"

"It was all kept very quiet, but I believe so."

"Then why did not the Earl of Ockendon do the same thing?"

"Sheer pride on the part of the Earl and the Viscount, Miss Webb. They neither of them wished to admit to the irresponsibility and stupidity of such an action.

"I think, too, the Duke of Dorset, who was not a rich man, was only too pleased that his daughter should make such an advantageous marriage before she was even presented at Court."

Zenobia could see what had happened.

She thought it was the kind of foolish pride that eventually was bound to end in disaster.

"Fortunately, there had been a death in the family very recently," Mr. Williamson went on, "which made a secret marriage seem less peculiar to the Social World than it would have been otherwise."

Zenobia was listening intently as he went on:

"When His Lordship came down from Oxford at the end of the term, the bride and bridegroom were presented here at the Castle to the family and were given their own apartments and their own servants in the West Wing."

Zenobia waited, knowing instinctively what had happened.

"His Lordship was too young for the responsibility of marriage," Mr. Williamson went on, "and Lady Briget, now the Viscountess, was, if I may say so, while very pretty, not very intelligent.

"They started to quarrel and, like most young people, were insensitive to the other's point of view."

Mr. Williamson seemed almost to falter as he said:

"Then came tragedy! After a quarrel which had started at dinner time in front of the servants and continued noisily when they went first to their Sitting-Room, then upstairs to their bedroom, Lady Briget died by falling out of a window!"

Zenobia gave a little murmur of horror.

"She was found not that night, but the next morning, and falling from a great height, she had died instantaneously."

Zenobia's voice was as low as Mr. Williamson's as she asked:

"But . . . surely . . . her husband did not . . . push her out as Lady Mary said?"

"He did nothing of the sort!" Mr. Williamson said firmly. "After they had quarrelled bitterly, His Lordship walked out of his wife's bedroom, and left the house by a side-staircase, where, unfortunately, nobody saw him.

"He went out into the garden and down to the lake, stayed there until one o'clock in the morning, then returned to the Castle by a different door from the way he had left it, and went to his own bedroom and fell asleep."

"Then why did Lady Mary . . ." Zenobia began.

Mr. Williamson held up his hand.

"Wait a minute, Miss Webb! When Her Ladyship was found, and there were a number of servants to tell His Lordship's father what had occurred earlier in the evening, the old Earl assumed that his son was to blame."

Zenobia looked surprised as Mr. Williamson went on:

"His present Lordship protested his innocence, describing exactly what had happened as I have just told you, but unfortunately nobody had seen him leave the house, and because he had come back by a different route, he had not seen his wife's body lying beneath her window in the court-yard, nor did anybody see him go up to bed."

"What about his valet?" Zenobia murmured.

"As it happened, his valet had an extremely bad cold and he had told the man he was to go to bed early and he would look after himself."

"So what happened?" Zenobia asked.

"By now the doctor who had been called to the Viscountess was aware of how she had died, and the late Earl was thinking it was his duty to send for the Chief Constable and tell him what had happened, when the gardener's daughter saved His Lordship from being sent before the Magistrates."

"How did she do that?"

"She had been meeting secretly a young man of whom her father and mother did not approve, and was brave enough to come forward. They had been courting down by the lake and when they saw the Viscount approaching had hidden together in the bushes.

"She described how he had stood for a long time staring into the water, almost as if he contemplated, she said, throwing himself in.

"Then he sat on the bank opposite to where they were hiding, thinking over, one presumes, the tragedy of his marriage, for about an hour."

"So that saved him!" Zenobia said.

Somehow she felt relieved and glad that the story had a happy ending.

"That was how he was saved from being brought to Trial for murder, and the Viscountess's death was declared 'Accidental.'"

"Then why should Lady Mary accuse him of such a terrible thing?" Zenobia asked.

There was silence and she thought Mr. Williamson was not going to tell her the truth.

Then at last, almost as if he forced the words from between his lips, he said:

"Lady Mary is resentful of her half-brother because not being a man she could not inherit the title and Estate."

"It seems incredible that she should feel like that," Zenobia said, "to the point where she would deliberately accuse her half-brother of a crime she must know he did not commit."

Again there was a pause before Mr. Williamson said:

"I am afraid her position has played on Lady Mary's mind for a long time, and now, since His Lordship's accident, she has assumed an authority to which she is not

91

entitled and which is very much resented by all who live here."

He hesitated before he added:

"She also tries, by every means she can, to set His Lordship's servants against him."

"I cannot believe it!" Zenobia exclaimed.

At the same time, she knew now that this was the peculiarity she had felt about Lady Mary.

Then a thought came to her and she asked:

"I can understand her feelings in a way, but why, when I am only His Lordship's secretary, should she be so anxious to be rid of me?"

"I should have thought that was obvious, Miss Webb!"

"Not to me!" Zenobia said. "But perhaps I am being very stupid."

"What Lady Mary has always been afraid of," Mr. Williamson explained, "is that His Lordship will marry again and have a son."

Zenobia stared at him.

Then she said:

"She must be crazy if she thinks that I could be in any way dangerous from that point of view!"

"As Her Ladyship has remarked, you do have a slight resemblance to the Viscountess, who was also fair-haired and very pretty," Mr. Williamson said.

"I wish I could reassure Lady Mary that she need have no fear of me on that score," Zenobia said firmly.

At the same time, she found herself hoping that this strange and twisted situation would not result in her having to leave the Castle.

She had found the perfect hiding-place.

A position which not only kept her busy, but was extremely interesting.

What was more, she knew she could do her job well.

Surely Lady Mary, who must be slightly unhinged with regard to her half-brother, could not force her to leave.

For no reason but that she resembled a woman who had been dead for eleven years.

Impulsively she said to Mr. Williamson:

"Help me . . . please . . . help me! I know I could very much enjoy working for His Lordship, and all these ridiculous ideas and tragedies are past, and have nothing whatsoever to do with me or my work."

"I agree with you, Miss Webb," Mr. Williamson replied. "At the same time, I think you will have to be careful, very careful indeed, where Lady Mary is concerned!"

Zenobia did not quite understand why he found it so serious.

But she was grateful to him for telling her the truth.

He made her feel that if it was in his power, he would protect her.

chapter five

WHEN the Earl eventually sent for Zenobia, it was getting late in the morning.

When she entered his Sitting-Room she understood the reason.

He was standing by the window fully dressed.

She gave an exclamation of surprise.

"I am proving to myself that I am well," the Earl said.

"I am so glad! It must be such a relief!"

The Earl sat down very carefully in a chair.

As if he wanted to avoid an answer to what she had just said, he asked:

"How many letters have you done?"

"All those that were on your list for India, and I have written down the names of a number of other people whom I think would be worth while for Your Lordship to approach.

Zenobia handed him the list as she spoke.

He looked at it, saying as he did so:

"I presume all these titles are correct?"

"They are taken from *The Golden Book of India*," Zenobia replied, "which, fortunately, you have in the Library. I think if we wanted to query any of the names I could write to the India Office."

"I can see you are very efficient, Miss Webb, which I appreciate," the Earl said briefly.

They then went on to discuss her supplementary list of Indians, some of whom were known to Zenobia, and some to the Earl.

Several times Zenobia noticed he was moving his leg uncomfortably.

Finally, as if he surrendered to the pain, he pulled a stool near to his chair and put his leg on it.

"Is your leg hurting you?" she enquired.

"If you want to know the truth," the Earl replied, "it is exceedingly painful, and it annoys me even more to admit that the doctors were right in warning me that it was a mistake to move it too soon."

Zenobia hesitated, then she said:

"I can, if you will allow me, attempt to heal it. It is something I learnt to do first in India, and later from a Bedouin Witch-doctor."

The Earl stared at her, then he said with a twist of his lips:

"This I do not believe! You have surprised me enough already, Miss Webb, and now, if you have magical powers, I shall be sure you are entirely a figment of my imagination!"

Zenobia rose to her feet.

"I make no promises," she said, "but I have been successful in the past, and when my father was in pain I could always remove it."

She spoke quite naturally of her father.

Then she wondered, as she had not mentioned him before, whether the Earl would notice that she had not said "my employer."

However, it appeared that the Earl was concentrating on himself.

He had not noticed her slip of the tongue.

"What do you want me to do?" the Earl asked. "I dressed this morning with the greatest difficulty, and I do not feel like doing it all over again."

Zenobia smiled.

"It is not like that," she said. "Just leave your leg where it is, lean back in your chair, and shut your eyes."

"Why?"

"Because I want you to concentrate on seeing a shaft of light pouring into your leg. I shall be doing that myself, and the healing process is more successful when the patient co-operates."

"What sort of light?" the Earl asked irritably. "And where does it come from?"

"I think you know the answer to that without my telling you," Zenobia replied. "You are too well-read not to know that light is life!"

Almost as if without further information she compelled him to think of it, the Earl remembered the words in the first chapter of the Book of Genesis in the Bible.

"God said, let there be light; and there was light."

He did not say anything, but did as Zenobia had asked by lying back in his chair and closing his eyes.

She stood beside him.

For a moment she just prayed, lifting her head upwards, her eyes closed.

Then she held both her hands over the injured part of his leg, which was above the knee, her fingers outstretched.

It was so that the Power, almost as if it were light, could pour through them.

There was absolute silence for some minutes.

Then the Earl opened his eyes and saw to his surprise that Zenobia was clearly not at all interested in him as a man.

She was completely lost in her concentration on pouring light, or rather life and healing, onto his leg.

It was something he had never seen a woman do before.

His intuition told him that what she was doing was very real to her.

She was concentrating on him as a *Saddhu* in India would concentrate on his soul, completely oblivious to anything that happened around him.

It had flashed through the Earl's mind, when Zenobia suggested she might try to heal him, that it was just another subterfuge—another woman attempting to attract him.

But he knew at this moment that Zenobia was genuinely in a world of her own.

It was one into which he could not enter, and dared not encroach.

He thought it was the strangest thing that had ever happened to him.

At the same time, he was aware that the pain which had been at first unpleasant, and then acute since he had been moving about, was unmistakably receding.

There was now a warmth in his leg which had not been there before.

As the warmth increased he could feel the pain gradually vanishing until it went completely.

He did not say so, but just sat watching Zenobia.

He was thinking she was the most extraordinary young woman he had ever met.

She was so different that he could still hardly believe that she was real.

Zenobia must have been standing by him for nearly ten minutes before she gave a little sigh.

It seemed to come from the very depths of her being, and she opened her eyes.

As she did so, she dropped her arms to her sides as if they were weary.

"Is that . . . better?"

Her voice was low and seemed to come from a long distance.

There was an anxiety in it which told the Earl she was a little unsure of her powers.

She was also afraid that he might laugh at her for attempting to do what was impossible.

"I can honestly say," he replied in his deep voice, "that at the moment I have no pain whatsoever in my leg!"

Zenobia's eyes lit up as if the light she had spoken of was caught in them.

"Is that true?" she asked. "The pain has really gone?"

"Completely!" the Earl smiled. "And now sit down and tell me how you do it."

Zenobia sat down as if she were glad to rest.

Then she replied:

"I do not have to make any explanations. You know what I believed would happen, and it has. I can only say a prayer of gratitude that you will not think I was trying to deceive you."

"I have heard of people being healed by the 'laying on of hands,'" the Earl said, "and I have heard of Witch-doctors making miracle cures in practically every Eastern country I have visited, but this is the first time I have seen one in action."

"Many Witch-doctors are impostors who just prey on the people who trust them," Zenobia said seriously. "But I have met two in whom I believe. In India there was one Healer who was obviously a very Holy man."

"And did he teach you?" the Earl enquired.

Zenobia shook her head.

"No, I believe that each one of us has the healing power within ourselves if we are strong enough to invoke the Life Force. It is, of course, life which heals, but the Greeks saw it as Light and they said that when every day Apollo crossed the sky he healed those who worshipped him."

The Earl was listening, because Zenobia spoke so simply and naturally.

He felt almost compelled to believe everything she told him.

Then, as if he wanted to prove her wrong, he began to move his leg from the stool.

He wanted to stand up to be quite certain the pain had really gone.

Zenobia stopped him.

"No!" she said. "Rest as you are for a little while. Remember that as your leg was badly injured, the Power will take time to work. But we have been successful so quickly that I think you will find in a few days you are completely healed."

"The Doctor told me it would take months!" the Earl remarked.

Zenobia did not argue, she merely smiled.

He knew she was thinking that doctors were only human while the Power that flowed through his leg was Divine.

It suddenly struck him as very strange that he seemed to be able to read her thoughts.

They were certainly very far from the banal and unoriginal thoughts he would easily have read in most other women.

"What is your Christian name?" he asked unexpectedly.

Because Zenobia was thinking of something else, she told the truth.

"Zenobia."

"Surely that is a very unusual name for an English girl?"

"Before I was born my father had always wanted to visit Palmyra, since he had found the history of Queen Zenobia fascinating, as I did as soon as I was old enough to understand."

"Tell me about her," the Earl commanded.

"Are you really interested?"

"Very."

"Well, for one thing," Zenobia replied, "I am not in the least like her, for she was dark, beautiful, energetic, and studied Greek Literature with a Philosopher."

"I am beginning to remember reading about her," the Earl remarked, "and I think before she married she was notable for her chastity."

"That is true," Zenobia said, "and perhaps that is why—"

She stopped.

She had been about to say that perhaps that was why she had been so shocked by the immorality of the Society women like her Stepmother.

Once again the Earl found himself reading her thoughts.

"Why should you," he asked, "worry your head about how other people lead their lives, when you are only just starting your own? If they are what you call 'bad,' they are not worth thinking about."

Zenobia stared at him.

It seemed as if once again her eyes held a strange light.

"You are right," she exclaimed, "completely right! I did not think about it that way before. It was very foolish of me to allow anything evil to intrude on my thoughts, which should concentrate only on everything that is beautiful and good."

She spoke in a rapt little voice as if the Earl had given her an inestimable gift.

He wondered if he had ever heard a woman so thrilled with anything that was not jewels.

"I am sure that is right," he said aloud, "and as you know, the Greeks changed the thinking of the world and emphasised that thought is much more important than action."

Zenobia clasped her hands together.

"I never expected to hear you say anything like that!" she said without thinking.

The Earl raised his eye-brows and she added quickly:

"Forgive me, that was very rude, but I did not imagine that anyone who lived in the Social World would understand."

"I think you must have met in London some very strange and undesirable people," the Earl remarked.

Zenobia looked away from him.

Then, as he was obviously waiting for a reply, she said after a moment:

"You have just...told me not to...think about... them."

"Then we will talk of something else," he said, "and perhaps that should be our work."

"Of course," Zenobia said, almost as if he had rebuked her.

She rose from the chair in which she had been sitting.

She picked up her notes which were on a table on the other side of the Earl.

As she did so, the Butler announced that luncheon was ready.

Very gingerly the Earl rose from his chair.

"Now I am going to test how successfully you have healed me," he said.

Zenobia cried out in protest.

"I am sure it is much too far for you to walk to the Dining-Room!"

"I have Your Lordship's chair ready," the Butler offered.

"I intend to walk!" the Earl said firmly.

Zenobia was worried.

At the same time, she knew when he spoke in that authoritative manner that he intended to have his own way.

He walked slowly, holding himself as an athlete should.

They reached the Dining-Room in silence and without mishap.

He sat down in the high chair at the head of the table.

Only then did Zenobia ask, as if she could no longer prevent herself from doing so:

"Are you all right?"

"I have no pain," the Earl replied.

She gave a cry of delight.

The servants were just handing them the first course when the door of the Dining-Room opened.

To Zenobia's surprise, Lady Mary came in.

"As I have seen so little of you, D'Arcy," she said to the Earl, "and you have omitted to invite me to visit you, I have decided to have luncheon with you."

There was only a faint pause before the Earl replied:

"What a good idea, Mary! And, of course, I am very pleased to see you!"

The servants hastily placed a chair for Lady Mary on the Earl's left.

They laid a place, and were tactful enough to serve her first before Zenobia.

To Zenobia's surprise Lady Mary made herself extremely pleasant.

She talked not only to her half-brother, but also to Zenobia.

She made no complaints about the household or the Estate.

She had, however, brought a kind of oppression with her, of which Zenobi was very conscious.

She could feel Lady Mary's dark eyes flickering over her.

When she spoke to her, Zenobia was acutely conscious that she was thinking that if she had followed her advice, she should have left by now.

"It is ridiculous! Absurd!" she told herself. "I will not think of it."

But it was something she could not help.

The moment coffee had been served, she said to the Earl:

"I am sure, My Lord, that Lady Mary wants to talk to you alone, and as I have a great deal of work to do, will you please excuse me?"

"Of course, Miss Webb, if that is what you wish," the Earl replied in a formal manner.

Zenobia was about to walk from the room when Lady Mary said:

"You have not forgotten what I told you, Miss Webb?"

"No, My Lady," Zenobia replied.

She reached the door.

She had an impulse to run as quickly as she could to somewhere where she could escape from the dark, piercing eyes of Lady Mary.

Zenobia had a strange feeling, although, of course, she knew it must be absurd.

Yet while she was talking so genially, she was willing

the Earl to murder *her* as she believed he had murdered his wife.

"She must be mad!" Zenobia told herself.

She was sure that living alone and unmarried had made her slightly unhinged.

At the same time, she was afraid, not that the Earl would murder her, for she was quite certain he would not do that, but that somehow Lady Mary would contrive that she would have to go away.

She could not leave what was a perfect hiding-place besides giving her work which she really enjoyed.

"Please, God, do not...let her...interfere," she prayed.

Then, almost as if he were beside her, she found herself talking to her father.

"Why can she not leave me alone, Papa?" she asked. "Supposing she does make it too difficult for me to stay, where shall I go and what shall I do?"

She almost had to force herself to look through Colonel Malleson's book for some more names rather than sit thinking of Lady Mary.

Of course Zenobia believed the account Mr. Williamson had given her.

At the same time, he had not explained why the Viscountess, unhappy though she might be, should have thrown herself out of the window.

What had she to gain by dying, however much her husband might annoy her.

She had in other respects a very pleasant and comfortable life.

If she was unhappy, she could have gone back to her own family or at least arranged with the Viscount that they should live apart.

There were a number of questions unanswered, Zenobia thought.

Then she told herself the Earl was right.

She should not be thinking of such unpleasant and ugly things.

Instead, she should be finding so much that was beautiful in the Castle.

She had not yet had time to look at the pictures which hung on the walls.

Nor to explore the State Reception Rooms which included, Lucy had told her, a large and very magnificent Ballroom.

'I must ask Mr. Hedges to show it to me,' Zenobia thought.

Then she started as the door of her Sitting-Room opened and Lady Mary came in.

"I hoped I would see you packing," she said reproachfully.

"You have been very kind, My Lady, in warning me," Zenobia said, "but I am finding my work here so absorbing that I do not wish to leave."

"How can you be so stupid?" Lady Mary asked. "As I have told you, your life is in danger. I saw my half-brother looking at you at luncheon, and because I know him so well, I am sure he is already thinking that, because you so closely resemble his wife, you too must die!"

She had come close to Zenobia as she spoke.

As she lowered her voice, Zenobia felt that what she said was very creepy.

She found herself shivering.

"I will think about it," she said quickly. "I promise you, My Lady, I will think about it, but I should have to make some explanation for leaving so unexpectedly."

"You could say that you have heard that a relation is

105

ill," Lady Mary suggested, "or you could go away for the day and not come back. If you have no money, I will give you some."

"No, I am quite all right, thank you," Zenobia replied.

She did not wish to be beholden to this strange woman.

"Then do as I tell you!" Lady Mary said. "Leave to-morrow or, if you are wise, to-night."

Quite suddenly Zenobia decided she would not be intimidated.

Mr. Williamson had said that the Earl had not killed his wife.

She would far rather believe him than Lady Mary.

"I think, My Lady," she said bravely, "I must make up my own mind and, quite frankly, I do not believe His Lordship wishes to murder me."

Lady Mary made an angry exclamation, but Zenobia went on:

"As I enjoy working for him and he finds me at the moment very helpful regarding the Exhibition, I am confident that he has no other idea than that I am a competent secretary."

As she spoke, her voice seemed almost to ring out the words.

Lady Mary's expression changed.

"Very well, Miss Webb," she said, "if you are so fool-hardy, then you must, of course, be prepared for the consequences. But you cannot say I have not warned you, and done my very best to save you."

"Yes, of course, and I am very grateful that you have thought of me so kindly," Zenobia said.

"It is not gratitude I want you to show," Lady Mary said, "but common sense!"

She walked away to the door.

When she reached it she looked back.

"I have warned you!" she said ominously, and was gone.

For a moment Zenobia felt as if she could not move.

Then she told herself it was absurd to be frightened.

She thought of how much she enjoyed talking to the Earl and of her success in healing his leg.

It was impossible to believe he could kill her on the flimsy excuse that she resembled his wife.

"I expect Lady Mary was a little mad before the tragedy, and afterwards it preyed on her mind," she told herself.

Nevertheless, she found it difficult to concentrate on her work.

The Earl was resting, so she went into the garden.

The flowers, the song of the birds, and the iridescent fall of water in a fountain were like a light from Heaven.

They swept away the depression that Lady Mary had left behind her.

Instead, Zenobia found herself enveloped by the beauty of it all.

When she returned to the house her heart was singing and her eyes were shining because she was happy.

"His Lordship's askin' for ye, Miss Webb," a footman said as she went back through the hall.

Zenobia hurried up to her room, collected her papers on *The History of the Native States*.

She ran down the corridor to the Earl's Sitting-Room.

She found him, as she expected, sitting in his arm-chair.

His foot was on the foot-stool.

"I am sorry," she said as she came into the room, "very sorry to be late, but I went into the garden and it was so beautiful that I forgot the time, and that I should have been on duty."

"That is a better excuse than any other you could have invented," the Earl said.

"I never lie if I can help it," Zenobia replied, "because, as my Nanny used to say when I was very young: 'One lie leads to another!'"

"I am sure my Nanny said the same thing!" the Earl replied.

Zenobia thought he was looking at her in a strange way.

It was as if he expected her to say something about Lady Mary.

Instead, she opened the book and started to add to the list she had already made.

It was of Maharajahs with Palaces in which there were ancient treasures that had never been shown in public.

The Earl listened, but she had the feeling his thoughts were elsewhere.

At last he said:

"That is enough, Miss Webb! I think we shall have represented India so well that the other parts of our Empire will be jealous!"

"I expect they will be anyway!" Zenobia replied. "The fact that the Queen is so interested in India, and so is the Prince of Wales, has not gone unnoticed by the rest of the world."

"I am prepared to take your word on that," the Earl said sarcastically.

Zenobia blushed.

"I must remember to be more subservient," she said to herself.

Yet it was difficult not to talk to the Earl as she had talked to her father, as if she were an equal.

When they had completed their notes on Ceylon, it was tea-time.

The Earl said:

"Mr. Williamson is coming to see me in a few minutes, Miss Webb, but I would like you to dine with me, and as this is my first day up, I think we should dine early, perhaps at seven-thirty?"

"Thank you, My Lord," Zenobia replied.

Then, when she would have gone away, she stopped and said:

"If Lady Mary is dining with you, perhaps it would be best for me to have dinner in my Sitting-Room?"

The Earl frowned.

"I have not invited my sister to dine with me, and as far as I know, she will be in her own apartments. I therefore expect you, Miss Webb, as part of your duties, to keep me company."

"Thank you, My Lord," Zenobia said hastily, and left him.

She walked towards her own rooms.

She decided as she did so that the Earl disliked his half-sister almost as much as she disliked him.

It was not surprising if she had warned other women who stayed at the Castle that her brother was a murderer.

Zenobia was quite certain that if she had done so, the ladies in question would undoubtedly have run to the Earl.

They would have told him what had been said and begged him for his protection.

If that was what had happened, it seemed extraordinary that he still kept her in the Castle.

'It is all very puzzling,' she thought, 'and at the same time unpleasant. It spoils what might have been the loveliest place I have ever stayed in.'

She suddenly realised that this was a very revolutionary thought.

She remembered how happy she had been with her father!

How could she possibly feel anything so overwhelming about a Castle she had never heard of until a week ago?

While its owner was a man she had just met?

She failed to find the answer.

She therefore sat down at her desk to start writing the letters that needed her attention.

"You've got very few evening-gowns, Miss!" Lucy said when it was time for her to change for dinner.

"I know," Zenobia replied, "but I was not expecting to dine anywhere so magnificent as this!"

"Well, anyway, Miss, you looks lovely in them," Lucy said impulsively, "an' I've asked for some flowers for you to put in your hair."

"That is kind of you," Zenobia said in surprise.

She thought it was something she might have thought of herself.

She remembered that her father had told her that in all the grand houses the ladies wore tiaras in the evening.

When the Prince of Wales was present he insisted on it.

Lucy produced a small bunch of orchids and a number of white carnations for Zenobia to choose from.

She chose the orchids. They were white, with touches of pink in them, which she thought were lovely.

They made her think of the orchids she had seen in Singapore and in Siam.

Then she hesitated.

"Perhaps His Lordship will think it strange that I am wearing his flowers without his permission!"

Lucy laughed.

"Oh, no, Miss, he won't think that! When there's house-parties at the Castle the gardeners send in flowers for everybody. Sprays for the ladies, buttonholes for the gent'men, and they takes their choice."

"What a lovely idea!" Zenobia exclaimed.

She now remembered that her father had told her of that custom.

But she had forgotten about it.

She arranged the orchids at the back of her head in the same way that Indian women wore *frangipani* blossoms.

There were a few more to pin at the front of her gown.

"They're much prettier than jewels, Miss!" Lucy exclaimed.

Zenobia agreed with her.

Then, looking at her reflection in the mirror, she said:

"I have never worn a tiara, and I should imagine it would be rather uncomfortable."

"You can't wear one 'til you're married, Miss," Lucy replied. "All the ladies as comes 'ere 'as them 'cause they're married."

"I never thought of that," Zenobia said. "Does His Lordship never entertain young girls?"

"Not since I've bin 'ere," Lucy said, "and the ladies as fancies 'im always 'as a 'usband somewhere in the background!"

Lucy giggled.

Zenobia was just about to say coldly that that was not the sort of thing she should say.

Then she remembered that Lucy was not thinking of her as one of the smart society women who were the Earl's guests.

She was just somebody who served His Lordship as she did herself and was paid for doing so.

It made her, as her father's daughter, feel strange. But she told herself she was really very lucky.

At least nothing would be expected of her.

The Earl as a man would not think of her as a woman who interested him.

'If he did, I would have to leave,' she thought.

She remembered again Sir Benjamin Fisher, and the

man who had walked down the passage with his arm around her Stepmother.

She thought suddenly that it was a mistake for her to wear flowers.

She would have taken the orchids from her hair.

Then she had thought that Lucy would be hurt.

"Anyway, the Earl will not notice me," she told herself re-assuringly. "He does not think of me like that."

She went downstairs to the Salon, where they were to meet before dinner.

She found him standing as she entered the room and he seemed larger and more overpowering than when he was in a wheel-chair.

She thought he was watching her as she crossed the room.

Unexpectedly, it made her feel shy.

As she reached his side he said:

"I am wondering how I can thank you for making me a different man from what I was last night."

She looked at him enquiringly, and he explained:

"You will hardly credit it, but my leg has not hurt me the whole evening, and I have been careful, as you told me to be."

"That is sensible," Zenobia said, "and perhaps you will need a little more healing to-morrow and the next day. After that, unless anything goes wrong, you should be your old self again."

"I feel that already," the Earl said. "There was nothing wrong with me when I left London, except that I had constant pain. Now it is no longer there, though I find it difficult to believe that you have been more effective than half-a-dozen Specialists!"

"I appreciate the compliment," Zenobia said, "but, please, may I ask you something?"

"Of course," the Earl replied.

She did not look at him as she said:

"Please . . . you will not . . . tell anyone that I . . . healed you?"

There was a silence, then the Earl said:

"I am interested to know why you should be secretive about it."

"It is not exactly a secret," Zenobia said, "but I feel if you tell anyone, they would be sceptical and perhaps think I had some ulterior motive in trying to heal you."

"I understand exactly what you are saying to me," the Earl replied, "and of course I will keep it a secret as you have asked me to do so. At the same time, I think the gift of healing is something so extraordinary and so unusual that you should not hide it away and remain anonymous."

"But that is exactly what I want," Zenobia said. "Like everything else, it is in many cases just a question of luck."

She gave a little sigh before she said:

"To be truthful, I have not healed many people, and I would not presume to think that I can always use the Power in which I believe as successfully as I have done with you."

"Have you asked yourself why you should have been so successful with me?" he asked.

It was a question that the Earl knew most women would answer not only with their lips, but by the light in their eyes.

They would also instinctively draw nearer to him.

But Zenobia answered seriously:

"What you have to convince yourself is that Your Lordship is a very strong and healthy person, and the healing came in answer to prayer from inside yourself and not from outside.

She spoke very positively as she added:

"The Power can work more quickly, one might say, than if one had first to change or eradicate something that was not merely physical but also mental."

It was an explanation which the Earl accepted as being not only clever but, he thought, genuine.

He said quietly:

"Then may I say once again, Miss Webb, I am very grateful."

At dinner with the servants waiting on them they talked about the Earl's pictures.

Zenobia plied him with questions about them.

At last he had to admit that he was stumped for an answer.

"I am only ashamed," he confessed, "that I have not had more time to study the pictures which hang in the Castle, and which I can remember since I was a child. Also the history of the artists who painted them and the models they used."

He looked at Zenobia for a long moment before he said:

"Perhaps that is what you, as a girl, should be doing— sitting for an artist as Botticelli painted Simonetta Vespucci as Venus or, as the Greeks called her, Aphrodite."

The servants had left the room.

For a moment Zenobia did not realise that the Earl was paying her a compliment.

She looked at him in surprise.

Then she saw an expression in his eyes that made her draw in her breath.

"You are very beautiful, Zenobia," the Earl said, "as I expect a great many men have told you."

For a moment Zenobia was almost hypnotised by the deep tone of his voice. As he spoke he reached out and put his hand over hers.

Then she suddenly realised that the Earl was speaking to her in the way that Sir Benjamin had done.

The men sitting on either side of Irene at the dinner-table had spoken in the same way.

It was what she most feared and despised.

With the swiftness of a frightened fawn, she pulled her hand from beneath the Earl's.

She rose to her feet.

"I think, My Lord," she said, "it is now . . . correct for me to . . . leave you to drink your . . . port."

The words came quickly from her lips.

Without looking at the Earl again, she ran from the room, closing the door sharply behind her.

He stared after her.

He knew he would not see her again that evening.

He told himself he had not only over-rated his own charm where women were concerned.

He had, instead, succeeded in being extremely foolish.

chapter six

ZENOBIA reached her bedroom.

She found her heart was beating tumultuously and she was breathless.

She sat down in an arm-chair and thought she had been extremely stupid.

She had behaved in what her father would have thought was an hysterical manner.

"I am sure the Earl was just being kind," she said, "and, of course, I have healed his leg and he is grateful."

She could almost hear her father talking to her.

He was saying that she could not go through life running away from every man who paid her a compliment.

Or of being afraid of them because she was a woman.

"I wish foolish, Papa," she said, "and I am sure the Earl will now think I am not the sensible and intelligent secretary he requires."

She debated with herself whether she should go downstairs and apologise.

But she thought that would be even more embarrassing.

Having collected a book from her Sitting-Room, she decided she would go to bed.

She hoped the Earl, too, would go to bed.

If he did too much, his leg would begin to hurt him again.

She found herself worrying.

She had not suggested he should be carried upstairs in his wheel-chair rather than walk.

She hoped he would remember not to make any hasty or complicated movements when he was undressing.

This occupied her thoughts for a long time.

Suddenly she realised she was sitting up in bed with the book open in front of her.

She had not read a single word.

"I will be more sensible to-morrow," she told herself.

As she said her prayers she prayed that she would not do anything to upset the Earl.

Most of all, that she would not have to leave because of Lady Mary's insinuation.

"It all seems very . . . complicated," she sighed before she went to sleep.

*   *   *

When Zenobia awoke, it was very early.

At the back of her mind she thought she might not be able to ride for much longer, so she went to the stables.

Once mounted, she galloped her horse until she felt all her difficulties had been blown away on the wind.

Immediately after breakfast she settled down to work on her letters.

Each one had to be different, each potential Exhibitor had to be addressed correctly.

This took her such a long time.

She realised with surprise that there had been no call from the Earl, and it was nearly half-past twelve.

She was sure he must be up by now, unless his leg was hurting him.

But, if that were so, surely he would have sent for her?

She wondered if she should find out from Mr. Williamson if anything was wrong.

Then a footman came to her Sitting-Room to say:

"'Is Lordship's compliments, Miss, an' 'e's had a number of engagements this mornin' which has prevented him from askin' for you, an' as 'is last caller's staying to luncheon, 'Is Lordship 'opes as you'll understand, an' 'ave your luncheon up 'ere."

The footman recited what he had to say as if he had learnt it by heart.

He gave a sigh of relief when he had finished.

"Of course I understand," Zenobia replied, "and I would like luncheon as soon as possible."

When she was alone she thought how disappointing it was that she could not be with the Earl.

She seemed to remember that yesterday when they were talking he had said that he had to see the Manager of the Estate.

Perhaps he was responsible for keeping the Earl so busy during the morning.

At the same time, she could not help wondering who was having luncheon with him.

A little later, having finished her own meal, she was just about to go into the garden.

She had reached the landing at the top of the stairs, when she saw a gentleman arriving in a Phaeton.

He was very smartly dressed.

As she waited instead of descending the stairs, he walked in through the front-door.

She heard the Butler say:

"Lord Ventnor, I think?"

"That is right," the gentleman replied. "His Lordship is expecting me to luncheon, but I am afraid I am late."

The Butler escorted him across the hall.

When he was out of sight, Zenobia ran down the stairs and into the garden.

She did not find the beauty of the syringa, the lilac, and the almond blossom quite as beautiful as she had done before.

She was thinking that she really lived now in a very different world from the Earl.

She was useful in keeping him company when he had no guests.

He did not want her when he was entertaining his friends.

It was, of course, ridiculous to be upset that she was excluded from the Dining-Room.

She had deliberately chosen to be a mere secretary.

She had never confided to him who she was.

She was sure he would have heard of her father and her standing would then be very different.

Yet, she told herself, she was again being extremely stupid.

At the moment the Earl had no idea that she was acceptable in the same society in which he himself moved.

Once he did, it would be impossible for her to remain with him at the Castle.

He had informed her slightly sarcastically that she was chaperoned by his half-sister.

But if as the Honorable Zenobia Chade she were staying with one of the most alluring, fascinating, and fêted men in the *Beau Ton*, she would certainly not be allowed to have luncheon or dinner with him alone.

Nor to spend many hours alone in his Sitting-Room.

There would have to be an older and preferably married woman with them.

'I am trying to "have my cake and eat it"!' Zenobia thought wryly.

She forced herself to enjoy the fountain in the herb-garden.

Also the beauty of a Grecian Temple which stood at the end of the shrubbery.

However, when she returned to her work she could not prevent herself from listening to hear when Lord Ventnor left.

Then she waited anxiously.

Although she would not admit it to herself, also excitedly for His Lordship's summons.

To her astonishment it did not come.

Although she had a large pile of letters to show him, there was no sign that he remembered either her or the Exhibition.

Despite every resolution to think of other things, she dressed for dinner earlier than usual.

She rang for Lucy and had her bath brought to her room an hour before her usual time.

Lucy was chattering away as she always did.

Zenobia was only half-listening as she dried herself in a big white Turkish towel.

There was a knock on the door.

She could hear one of the footmen talking to Lucy.

He seemed to have quite a lot to say.

Zenobia had become very curious by the time the maid shut the door and returned to her.

"'Is Lordship's compliments, Miss," she said, "and 'e asks that you should be informed that the Lord Lieutenant and his wife is arrivin' with their daughter. They'll be dinin' with 'Is Lordship to-night, an' 'e 'opes you'll understand, and enjoy your dinner up 'ere."

For a moment Zenobia was so disappointed that she could not speak.

Then she realised Lucy was waiting for reply.

In what she hoped was an indifferent voice, she said:

"Of course I understand, and as I have so much work to do, it will give me a chance to have things ready for His Lordship to-morrow."

"The Lord Lieutenant, the Marquess of Darlington, must be a-gettin' very old," Lucy said. "The last time 'e come 'ere 'e was totterin' on two sticks. I was watchin' 'im from the window, an' I was afraid 'e was goin' to fall down the steps!"

"What is his daughter like?" Zenobia enquired.

"Oh, she's ever so pretty, Miss, we all admires Lady Cecelia, an' she's ever so much liked in th' County."

Zenobia drew in her breath.

The Lord Lieutenant and his wife had been asked to dinner and to bring their daughter with them.

Was there any chance of the Earl considering Lady Cecelia as his wife?

She could not think why the idea came to her.

Especially after Lucy had said that all the ladies in whom the Earl was interested were married.

Yet it seemed a reasonable supposition.

Especially if Lady Cecelia, as Lucy had said, was very pretty.

"It would certainly be a sensible marriage for the Earl," Zenobia reasoned, "since he has to marry again some time, so as to have an heir for this wonderful house and everything he possesses."

It was then she was aware that the idea gave her a strange sensation.

It was one she had never known before.

It was painful and for a moment she did not understand what she was feeling.

Then suddenly she knew, although it seemed completely impossible, that she was jealous.

The pain of it continued after Lucy had left her and she had moved into the Sitting-Room.

A table had been laid by one of the footmen.

He was waiting to serve the silver dishes that had been placed on a side-table.

As Zenobia sat down she felt as if it would be impossible to force a mouthful between her lips.

The delicious food cooked by the Earl's Chef might have been sawdust for all she could taste of it.

She took a minute helping of everything she was offered and messed it about on her plate without eating it.

Finally dinner was finished and she was alone.

She opened the window to stare out at the dusk that was just receding into darkness.

She could see the first evening star glittering in the last vestige of light that was left of the setting sun.

It was so beautiful.

Yet it seemed to hurt her more than she was hurt already.

In a way she deliberately tried not to understand.

"How can I be so foolish, so idiotic?" she asked herself.

Then, almost as if the darkness outside told her the truth, she knew she was in love—in love with the Earl!

And he was not in the least interested in her except as a competent secretary for the Exhibition.

It was then she faced the future.

The moment all the letters were finished there would be no reason for her to stay any longer.

The Earl would have no further need of her services.

He had told her there were a number of people in London already waiting for each Exhibit to arrive.

They would be numbered and stored until they could be moved into the Royal Albert Hall.

"I cannot love him!" she told herself frantically. "It is ridiculous, when I despise the kind of life he leads, and the women he fancies, who are, I am sure, exactly like Stepmama."

But it was not the logic of the mind she was combating.

It was the beating of her heart and a feeling that was different from anything she had felt before.

It was indisputably love—the love she had never expected to find.

She had known the Earl for only a short time.

Yet she knew that for her he filled the world.

There was only his face, his eyes, and the sound of his voice. Nothing else was of any importance.

"How can I be such a fool, such an idiot?" Zenobia asked herself angrily. "I have heard of the women who pursue him whether he wants them or not. I have seen the way in which the Social World in which he reigns supreme behaves, the men seducing each other's wives, and ladies committing adultery with other women's husbands."

She tried to reason it out to herself.

Yet she could do nothing to assuage the emotions she could not control.

Whether he was good or bad, she loved the Earl, and she was now ridiculously jealous of the girl he was talking to downstairs.

"She will love him now and, if he marries her, she will still love him to distraction, however unfaithful he may be, however badly he treats her!"

She tried to make herself feel better, thinking that the

Earl would sooner or later be enticed away from his wife's side by a younger edition of Irene.

But that did not help, did not make her feel anything but an irrepressible yearning to be with him.

She wished to talk to him.

She longed to hear again that strange note in his voice when last night he had said she was beautiful.

"How can I have been such a fool as to run away from him?" she asked herself now despairingly.

She wished frantically as so many women have wished before that she could put back the clock.

"If he had just kissed me once," she whispered as she looked at the evening star, "I would have something to remember."

It was then she told herself that to save her pride she would have to leave the Castle.

How could she stay and watch him think of marrying Lady Cecelia?

Or anyone else for that matter, and not be crucified over and over again?

"I will go away to-morrow morning," she decided.

She knew she was running away not from the Earl but from herself.

She told Lucy, who was putting out her night things in the next room, that she would put herself to bed.

There was no reason for her to wait up for her.

"Are you sure you can manage, Miss?" Lucy asked. "I don't mind however late you rings."

"It is very sweet of you, Lucy," Zenobia answered, "but I really have some work that will keep me busy for hours, and it will worry me if I think you are keeping awake for me."

"You can manage to undress, Miss?"

"Of course I can," Zenobia smiled. "I have always looked after myself until now."

She thought of how when she was travelling with her father she had seldom had anybody to help her.

She was, in fact, proud of being so self-sufficient.

"Oh, well, good-night then, Miss," Lucy said, "but don't go tirin' yourself out. I expects you'll want to ride in th' mornin'."

"Yes, of course," Zenobia replied.

She knew, as she spoke, the only way she could get away without explanations.

It would be to leave very early before the Earl was called.

It was fortunate that he was not well enough yet to ride.

She had already learnt that he always rode before breakfast, as she did.

She was sure he was looking forward to exercising his magnificent stallions of which even the grooms were nervous.

It was agonising to think that now she would never have the opportunity of riding with him.

But if she stayed even for a few days longer, she might easily betray what she felt about him.

The resulting humiliation was too degrading to contemplate.

Mr. Williamson had warned her.

She had been so confident that she would not fall in love with the Earl like all the other idiotic women he knew.

As soon as Lucy had left, Zenobia locked the door leading into the passage.

She pulled her trunk from the cupboard in her bedroom, where it had been stacked away.

It was lucky she had brought so little luggage.

She was sure any more trunks would have been taken away to some attic.

There she could not easily get them back without explanations as to why she wanted them.

As it was, she knew it would not take her long to pack.

She would have to leave her father's books behind.

She could perhaps send for those later on, when she had found herself somewhere else to live.

Then she asked herself where she could go and had no answer.

However, it did not really matter.

All she was concerned about at the moment was to escape from the Castle.

She could not be near the Earl and love him in a way she thought no other woman had loved him before.

It was not just because he was a man and the most handsome and attractive one she had ever seen.

It was because, as in her ability to heal him so quickly, there was an affinity between them.

It was a part of the mind and the soul rather than of the body.

It was something spiritual and in a way perfect.

She knew it would be impossible to explain her love in words to the Earl, or to anybody else.

She had known, she thought, almost from the first moment she saw him that they had met in other lives.

Although she would not admit it to herself, they were part of each other.

That was why it had been so easy to be with him, to talk to him as an equal.

To find everything he said or thought had an echo within herself.

It was love, the supreme love that her father had had for her mother, but had never found again.

Where the Earl was concerned, he would never understand that was what she felt for him.

It was not just he possessive love that other women had given him.

It had made them, as he had said himself, 'moon round,' and want to touch him.

'I love him as I love the beauty of the stars,' she thought. 'The stars are always out of reach, but one would miss them if they were not there'.

She packed her box, putting everything in except for the coat and gown in which she would travel.

The evening-dress which she was wearing could be added when she undressed.

She got to her feet thinking she might as well go to bed so that she would wake very early.

She had to send for a carriage in which she would leave.

She had already decided she would drive to the nearest Posting Inn.

There she would send the carriage back, then hire one to carry her—where?

Here her thoughts came to an end.

For some time she could not think, not knowing England, where she should go.

Then she decided the sensible thing would be to return to Devonshire.

At least Mr. Bushell would be there.

He would, she felt sure, help her.

Moreover, there would be a number of people who remembered her father and who would perhaps assist her to find employment.

There was always the fear that Irene might try to find her.

Sir Benjamin, if he was interested enough, might make the journey to look for her.

She was sure, however, they would not look very hard.

She could certainly make Mr. Bushell keep the secret of where she was until all the danger was past.

It suddenly struck her how pathetic it was that she had so few friends to turn to when she was desperate.

Also, unlike most people, very few relatives.

"It is no use being sorry for myself," she said defiantly. "I have been lucky enough to come here, and perhaps I shall be lucky again."

Then she knew that never, never again would she find anyone like the Earl.

Although it seemed far-fetched to think such a thing, she knew he was the one man in her life who would always matter.

It would be impossible to find somebody to take his place. Or even a man she could tolerate.

She knew that only the Indians would understand that this was her *Karma*.

Everybody in the West would think she was over-imaginative.

Just a silly woman who had simply become infatuated with a man who was better-looking than any of his contemporaries.

"Perhaps we shall meet again in another life," Zenobia told herself, "and then things might be different."

It was, however, a very poor consolation for what she was feeling now.

She had an insane impulse to wait until the Earl was alone, and then tell him all her secrets.

She would tell him who she was, and what she felt.

She would make him understand that her love for him was very different from what any woman could ever have felt for him.

But she told herself he would only laugh.

Once again he would complain to Mr. Williamson that another woman was making a fool of herself.

It was then she heard a sound outside.

Looking along the side of the house from her bedroom window, she could see a carriage had drawn up outside the front-door.

Because of the angle at which her window was situated, she had to lean out a little way to see clearly.

A man, who was obviously the Lord Lieutenant, was moving on two sticks.

With the assistance of a footman on either side of him, he went down the flight of steps from the front-door.

He was followed from the house by a lady who was obviously his wife.

Her tiara glittering in the light and a fur-trimmed wrap clasped around her.

She stood for a moment at the top of the steps talking to the Earl.

Now Zenobia could see him quite clearly as his face was turned in her direction.

She felt her heart give a leap.

Then it turned over and over in her breast.

She could feel the Power within her winging its way to him.

It seemed astonishing that he was not aware of it.

But he merely kissed the Marchioness's hand before she followed her husband into the carriage.

Now the Earl was speaking to a girl whom Zenobia knew was Lady Cecelia.

She could not see her clearly because she was talking to the Earl and had her back to her.

But Zenobia saw she had dark hair and was wearing a white gown which glittered when she moved.

Round her shoulders was a white cape trimmed with what Zenobia thought must be ermine.

She was tall and slim, and moved gracefully.

After saying good-bye to the Earl, she ran down the steps and into the carriage.

Then as they drove off, the Earl turned and walked back through the lighted doorway into the hall.

"That is the end!" Zenobia told herself.

Then, because she could not help it, she whispered to the night air:

"Good-bye, my love, my only love, good-bye!"

She felt the tears come into her eyes and wiped them away angrily.

Then she found herself praying that the Earl would find happiness.

That he would have no more injuries or pain when she was not there to heal him.

Perhaps sometimes he would think of her with kindness.

It was a very unselfish prayer.

At the same time, Zenobia was aware that her whole body was pulsating with her love for him.

She did not leave the window, but stood looking out.

She was feeling the beauty of it, but not actually seeing it with her eyes.

The stars were coming out one by one.

The moon was rising up the sky, throwing its silver light on to the lake.

But all she could see was the Earl's face and hear his deep voice saying:

"You are very lovely, Zenobia!"

*   *   *

It was a long time later than Zenobia realised she was feeling a little cold.

She turned from the window to go back into the room.

Her open trunk was waiting for her.

There were only two candles alight by her bed.

They had been enough until now for her to see what she was packing.

She thought the dark shadows in the room make it gloomy, and was like her thoughts.

She put the candles on her dressing-table before she undressed.

As she was about to do so, she glanced at the clock on the mantelpiece.

It was nearly midnight.

The Lord Lieutenant and his wife and daughter had not been late in leaving.

She had therefore spent a long time praying and thinking of the Earl.

"I must go to bed," she told herself, "or I will never wake before five o'clock, when the rest of the household will be aroused."

It was then in the silence of the night that she heard a sound.

It made her start and hold her breath.

She was aware that somebody was outside her door.

It had been only a faint creak, or perhaps the movement of a foot.

Yet she had heard it, and it alerted her so that she stood still, listening.

She knew that two night-watchmen patrolled the lower part of the Castle.

They never came up to the First Floor in case they should disturb those asleep.

Yet she was sure that there was somebody outside her door.

Then slowly and silently she saw the handle turn.

For a moment, she could not believe it.

Then as she stared, she saw in the light of the two candles by the bed the handle being turned again.

She thought, too, that whoever was outside was also pushing at the door, trying to force it open.

It was then that everything that Lady Mary had said to her flashed through her mind.

She could hear the older woman's voice saying ominously:

"I have warned you!"

The handle turned again and Zenobia wanted to scream.

Whoever was outside was trying to enter her room silently and surreptitiously.

Who else would want to come in except the Earl intending to kill her?

Every nerve in her body tingled with fear.

She stood paralysed with shock, staring at the handle until her eyes ached.

There was one last push at the door.

When it refused to open, it sounded as if somebody was walking cautiously away.

She heard their footsteps retreating.

As she listened she knew they were going in the direction of the Earl's Master Bedroom at the far end of the corridor.

It was true then, true what Lady Mary had said.

He intended to kill her because she resembled his first wife!

He was a murderer who had never been caught and she was his next victim!

She felt herself go limp and faint with the horror of it.

As she realised she was trembling, there was another sound, and this time it was in her Sitting-Room.

Suddenly, with a terror that seemed to strike through her

like forked lightning, she remembered she had not locked that door.

Nor had she locked the communicating door which led into her bedroom near one of the windows.

Now she knew her only chance of survival was to lock that door as well.

But before she could do so, it was too late.

She heard a sound as if somebody had inadvertently knocked against a chair.

Then there was a footstep.

She realised the Earl's hand must be on the handle of the communicating door.

With a cry that seemed to die in her throat, she rushed across the room to the door which led into the corridor.

She unlocked it and fumbled at the handle.

As frantically she pulled the door, she heard the communicating door open.

Somebody came into the bedroom.

Without looking back she ran desperately to the top of the stairs.

She thought first that she would run out through the front-door.

Then she remembered it would be closed and bolted.

She thought that by a miracle she might find Mr. Williamson still in his office.

He was the only person she could trust, the only person who would understand.

She rushed down the stairs, holding up the front of her skirt so that it would not make her stumble.

She reached the marble hall.

The lights were dim, but she could still see her way.

As she went she could hear footsteps hurrying down the passage behind her.

Her unlocked and open door would have revealed where she had gone.

She wanted to scream but she was too breathless.

As she tore across the hall, the door of the Salon opened and the Earl stood there.

He was silhouetted against the light.

His appearance was so unexpected that Zenobia came to a sudden halt.

Her breath was coming intermittently from between her lips.

Her breasts were heaving with the speed at which she had run and the agony within her.

He was there, not pursuing her, and she loved him!

She ran forward to throw herself against him.

Incoherently, in a voice he could hardly hear, she faltered:

"I . . . I . . . thought you . . . were trying to . . . k-kill me!"

His arms went round her.

As they did so, there was a sharp scream from the top of the stairs.

The Earl turned his head in the direction of the sound.

Without moving away from him, Zenobia did the same.

In a voice that was frenzied and wildly insane Lady Mary screamed:

"I will kill you! I will kill you for trying to marry him. The Castle is mine—do you hear? —mine, and no one else shall—have it!"

She was shouting from the upstairs landing which overlooked the hall.

Now she came to the top of the stairs and both the Earl and Zenobia could see her.

She was wearing a dark gown and carrying something sharp and glittering in her right hand.

"Where have you gone?" she screamed. "If you think

you can hide from me, you are mistaken! I am going to kill you because I know what you are after! I will kill you as I killed Briget. Then you will be dead—do you understand—dead—and so will he!"

She laughed and it was a frightening, obscene sound.

"He will die, as he should have died before," she went on, "and I will be the—owner of the Castle! I will take my—rightful place and it will not matter whether I am—a man or a woman—it will be mine—as it always should have been—as the oldest child."

She was talking to herself rather than her prey.

Zenobia clung to the Earl.

She was aware that Bateson the Butler had appeared from one passage and Mr. Williamson had come from the other.

It was then that they hesitated, wondering what they should do.

Lady Mary suddenly gave a scream that was even louder.

It seemed to echo up into the ceiling and round the great hall.

"I am going to kill you!" she shouted. "Kill you—and when you are dead—I shall be the Queen of the Castle—as is my right!"

On the last word she threw herself forward as if to run down the stairs.

The pointed dagger she held in her right hand glimmering in the candlelight.

But as she reached the third step, moving madly, almost as if she thought she could fly, her foot caught in her skirt.

There was a different scream from those she had made before.

She screamed with fear as she fell forward, rolling head-over-heels.

She crashed down the stairs, sliding finally off the bottom step onto the marble floor.

As if he were suddenly galvanized into action, the Earl would have moved towards her.

But as he tried to do so, Zenobia gave a murmur of horror and hid her face against him.

Mr. Williamson and Bateson were already running to the fallen body.

Instead of going with them, the Earl picked Zenobia up in his arms and carried her into the Silver Salon behind him.

He put her down so that he could shut the door.

He realised as he did so that she was crying, and he put his arm round her again.

"It is all right," he said gently. "This should never have happened. I should have sent her away a long time ago."

"I . . . I thought it was . . . y-you," Zenobia sobbed. "She . . . she told me . . . you were going to . . . k-kill me!"

He heard the horror in her voice.

He half-led, half-carried her to the sofa by the fireplace.

He sat her down, still holding her against him.

She could only sob helplessly.

"How could you think such cruel and wicked things about me?" he asked quietly and gently.

"She was . . . so insistent that you . . . intended to k-kill me . . . because she said . . . I . . . resembled your wife."

It was difficult to speak, but the Earl heard her.

"Now we know who really killed my wife. I was always certain that was what had happened, but I had no proof of it."

"Y-you . . . knew?"

"There was nobody else who had anything to gain by Briget's death. I had always known that Mary was insanely

136

jealous that because I was the boy I had inherited the Castle, while she was the first child of my father."

Zenobia gave a deep sigh.

Then she raised her face to the Earl's and said:

"I . . . I am . . . s-sorry."

Her eye-lashes were wet with tears and there were tears, too, on her cheeks.

Her mouth was trembling.

She looked so lovely that the Earl could only stare at her before he said:

"How could you think for one moment that I could kill someone I loved?"

For a moment, Zenobia did not understand.

Then very gently, as if he were afraid to frighten her, his arms tightened and his lips were on hers.

For a moment she could not believe it was happening.

She felt as if the moonlight flashed through her whole body and she knew it was the light that had healed him.

It was the Power that existed in them both and which made them closer than they had been before.

She was aware that it was the most perfect thing that had ever happened.

He kissed her until she thought there was nothing in the world but him.

She had forgotten Lady Mary, and her unhappiness.

Everything except the miraculous, unbelievable ecstasy he awakened in her.

Only when he raised his head did she say in a voice that seemed like the song of a lark:

"I . . . love you . . . I love . . . you!"

"How can you have done this to me?" the Earl asked. "I love you, my darling, and it is something I have never known before, something I thought I would never find."

"Do you . . . really love me?"

"The way I love you is so different that it is going to take a very long time to explain it," the Earl replied. "In fact, I think that is something you must do."

"It . . . cannot be . . . t-true!" Zenobia said in a little voice that broke.

He did not answer; he only kissed her again.

He kissed her until she knew she was not only looking at the stars, but touching them.

She had not only found her *Karma*, but so had he.

They were one, completely and indivisibly.

It was what she had thought would be impossible ever to find.

chapter seven

A little while later the Earl said:

"I think, my precious, I must go and see what is happening, but you are to stay here until I come back."

"I . . . will do . . . that," Zenobia answered.

As if he could not prevent himself, he kissed her again.

Then he walked resolutely from the room and closed the door firmly behind him.

Zenobia felt that she must be living in a dream.

What had happened could not be true.

When she had realised that she loved the Earl but was certain that he did not care for her, she had meant to go away.

She wanted to hide because she could not endure the misery of being with him knowing he might marry somebody else.

Now he had said he loved her!

Suddenly she remembered that although he had said he loved her, he had not asked her to marry him.

For the first time there was a question mark over the wonder and ecstasy he had aroused in her.

Feeling she could not keep still, she walked across the room.

She pulled back the damask curtains and opened one of the casement windows.

Once again she was looking out into the night.

Now the stars filled the sky with their brilliance.

The moonlight turned the garden into a fairy-land.

"It is true . . . it is true . . . he loves me!" she told herself reassuringly.

Yet still she was afraid.

It was only a few minutes before the Earl returned.

To Zenobia, waiting for him seemed an eternity.

When she heard him coming into the room she turned round.

Because she could not prevent herself, she ran towards him.

He put his arms around her and held her close against him.

"Is everything . . . all . . . right?" she asked in a frightened little voice.

"Everything!" he answered.

He drew her to where she had been looking out of the window.

Then he said in his deep voice:

"I love you, and nothing shall ever frighten you again."

She felt her heart give a throb of happiness, but there was still a question in her mind.

Looking out of the window, the Earl said:

"Williamson and Bateson have taken Mary upstairs and laid her on her bed."

"She is . . . dead?" Zenobia asked in a whisper.

"She broke her neck in the fall and died instantly," the Earl replied. "She therefore suffered no pain."

Zenobia gave a sigh and he went on:

"Williamson thinks the doctor will believe she has died of a heart-attack and there will therefore be no scandal. Of course Williamson and Bateson will never reveal to anybody what has happened here to-night."

"Can you really trust them not to?" Zenobia asked.

The Earl looked down at her and smiled.

"I trust them in the same way that I trust you, my precious. Williamson has been with me ever since I was very young, and Bateson has been at the Castle for thirty years. They are far more worried about my good name and that of the family than I am!"

His arms tightened as he said:

"Now we can think about ourselves, and how soon we can be married."

Zenobia looked up at him and he saw the starlight in her eyes.

"Married?" she repeated.

"I cannot imagine that you are going to refuse me!" the Earl said.

There was a hint of laughter in his voice.

"But . . . you know nothing about me, and I have not yet told you what you call my 'secrets.'"

"They are not important," the Earl said positively. "I know that you love me, and my love for you is very different from anything I have ever imagined, or thought I would be so fortunate as to find."

He spoke with a sincerity which made the tears come into Zenobia's eyes.

"Are you . . . really saying that to me?"

"I have a great deal more to say," the Earl replied, "but it is easier to kiss you!"

His lips were on hers and once again he carried her up to the stars.

It was impossible to think.

She could only feel that not merely her body was his but her heart, her soul, and her mind.

Nothing else was of any consequence.

After what seemed a long time, the Earl said:

"I am being very selfish. You have had a shock and I should have given you something to drink."

"I do not want ... anything except your ... kisses," Zenobia murmured.

He kissed her again, and it was a long, passionate kiss.

Then resolutely he drew her back to the sofa.

He left the window open so that they could still see the stars.

"I have thought of what we must do," he said quietly, "and I think you will agree that my plan is sensible."

"What are you ... suggesting?" Zenobia asked.

It was difficult to think clearly when she was so close to him.

She could feel the magnetism of him.

It was so strong that only with an effort could she concentrate on what he was saying.

As if he felt the same, he looked away from her as he said:

"Mary will be buried in the family vault and I have to be present at the Funeral. So I suggest ..."

Zenobia gave a little cry which interrupted him, and she said:

"You are ... sending me away? Oh ... please ... I cannot leave you!"

The Earl smiled.

"Do you think I would allow you to do that, even if you wanted to? No, my darling, you will stay here with me in the Castle, but I think it would be a mistake for any of my relatives, and there are a great number of them, to see you."

She looked up at him and saw an expression in his eyes that had never been there before.

She knew it was love.

"You are not to think," he said quietly, "that I am not proud of you, or that I do not want to show you off to the whole world as my wife."

Zenobia drew in her breath.

"It is just," he continfued, "that I am thinking of your reputation and I do not intend to give anyone any grounds for talking about you except with admiration and respect."

Zenobia's eyes were shining, but she did not interrupt.

He went on:

"What I want you to do is to work as fast as you can on the Exhibition, so that we shall not need to think any more about it. I am sure you can finish those letters by the time the Funeral is over."

Zenobia nodded her head.

She did not speak, and he continued:

"Then we will be married very quietly here by my private Chaplain, and the only persons present will be Williamson and Bateson, whom we can trust."

He kissed her forehead and went on:

"Then we will go away on our honeymoon, and after our return we will announce our marriage to the world and I will present you, my darling, as the most beautiful Countess of Ockendon there has ever been!"

Unconsciously Zenobia gave a little shudder.

"I do not want to be . . . presented to anyone . . . but I do want to be with . . . you."

"That is what you will be."

Then in a different voice Zenobia said:

"How can you plan all this and make it sound so . . . wonderful when you do not even . . . know who I . . . am?"

"I know you are somebody I have looked for all my life,

who has been with me in other lives," the Earl said very quietly, "and will be with me for all eternity."

Zenobia gave a sigh of sheer joy.

She hid her face against him.

"If only Papa could hear you say that," she whispered. "It is what he always ... wanted for me, but I thought it was ... impossible that there could be a ... man like you in the ... whole world!"

"Is that why you were determined never to get married?" the Earl asked.

"How could I marry ... any man who was not ... you?"

"That is exactly what I have been saying to myself," he said. "Will you tell me now, my precious, why you have run away and why you have such a hatred of everything that is Social?"

Zenobia drew in her breath and raised her head.

"My father was ... Lord Chadwell."

The Earl stared at her.

"Chadwell, the great traveller? Of course I know of him, but I had no idea he had a daughter."

"You have heard of Papa?"

"I heard of him in almost every country I have visited. I have also heard the story of how he walked out on his second wife because he was shocked by her behaviour."

"Do people ... really know ... that?"

"Some of my older relatives have never liked Lady Chadwell, and disapprove of her behaviour."

"That is what I do too," Zenobia said. "I feel she has ... defamed my ... mother's memory."

"So your father took you away with him!" the Earl said as if he must get the story clear. "Surely you were very young?"

"I was nine," Zenobia replied, "but I was already aware that my Stepmother was making my father very unhappy.

144

Then one day he told my Nurse to pack my things and, before anybody could have any idea that we were leaving, we were in a ship on our way to Constantinople!"

The Earl smiled.

"So that is how it all started!"

"It was very, very wonderful going to strange places with Papa, meeting unusual people and, because he was so clever, just being with him."

"I wish I had known him," the Earl said, "but I am very thankful to know his daughter."

He put his hand under Zenobia's chin.

He turned her face up to his as he asked:

"How can you be so ridiculously lovely, and at the same time so clever that your brain dazzles me just as much as your eyes do."

"Perhaps you will . . . get bored with me."

The Earl knew she genuinely had this fear and he said quietly:

"It would be impossible to be bored with one's self. You are a part of me, Zenobia, and we are joined together by the Power in which we both believe, which you have proved can heal me. How could it be possible for me to live without you?"

He was saying things that Zenobia thought she would never hear from a man.

She gave a murmur of happiness and whispered:

"All I know is that . . . I love you."

"As I love you!" the Earl said. "But go on telling me, my darling, what happened, and why you came here in the first place."

Zenobia told him how she and her father had come back from their travels because he wished to write a book, how they had lived for nearly a year in Devonshire before he died.

"He made a Will leaving me everything he owned," she said, "but I found there was no money left in the Bank because my Stepmother had spent it all. She had also mortgaged the house in London."

"How could she do anything so wicked?" the Earl asked. "But I always understood she was very rich."

"I think now that she has spent Papa's money," Zenobia said, the colour rising in her cheeks, "she depends on other men to . . . provide for . . . her."

The Earl thought this was undoubtedly true, but he did not say so.

Zenobia continued:

"She told me that as I was penniless, she would find me a husband and get rid of me as . . . quickly as . . . possible."

The way Zenobia spoke, a little shiver going through her, made the Earl say angrily:

"Was there some man she thought suitable for that position?"

Zenobia nodded, and although she could not look at him, she answered:

"He . . . was called . . . Sir Benjamin Fisher."

"That lecherous bounder," the Earl said scornfully. "Thank God, my darling, you ran away."

"I went to the Agency in Mount Street which Mr. Williamson had approached to find you a secretary who spoke Urdu and other Eastern languages. I was the only applicant who could offer such qualifications."

The Earl laughed.

"I thought I was asking the impossible, and when you appeared I was convinced it was a trick of some sort! I was sure no one could be so breath-takingly lovely, and at the same time able to speak languages or to have travelled in such unusual places."

"I knew I had surprised you," Zenobia said. "And if I

had not been so afraid of losing the job, I would have told you I thought it insulting that you were so sceptical."

"And now you know that I believe you, and like a miracle you have come into my life when I least expected it."

As if she felt she must be frank, Zenobia said:

"I . . . I had decided to run away from you . . . to-morrow. In fact . . . I had packed my . . . trunk, which was why I was not yet . . . undressed when . . . Lady Mary . . . came to . . . kill me."

"You were running away?" the Earl asked in surprise. "But—why?"

Zenobia hid her face against his shoulder.

He held her very close against him.

He did not speak, but she knew he was waiting for the answer to his question.

"When I realised that I . . . loved you," she whispered, "and it was the true love which Papa had for my mother and which came from God . . . and therefore could not be spoilt . . . I was sure you would never . . . love me . . . and so I had to . . . go away."

"I loved you from the first moment I saw you," the Earl said, "and because we are so close to each other and I can read your thoughts, I was aware that you not only hated everything to do with my social life, but you were also afraid of me as a man."

"That is . . . true . . . and . . . although I loved you . . . I was also jealous!"

"Jealous?" the Earl repeated in surprise. "But of whom?"

He could hardly hear the words as Zenobia faltered:

"Lady . . . Cecelia!"

For a moment he was still.

Then he laughed.

Because it was not what she had expected, she looked up at him in astonishment.

"I am laughing, my precious," he said, "because it is such a ridiculous idea. And yet I can understand you felt the Lord Lieutenant had an ulterior motive in bringing his wife and daughter to dine with me to-night."

"I was . . . told that she is . . . very pretty," Zenobia said defensively.

"She is!" the Earl agreed. "At the same time, the last few days all I have been able to see is a little pointed face, huge, very expressive dark blue eyes, and lips which were made for my kisses."

Zenobia could see the look on his face and blushed as he went on:

"The Lord Lieutenant certainly had a reason for coming here to-night, and he especially asked if we could dine alone."

Zenobia listened as the Earl went on:

"He came to tell me that he is a sick man and his duties have become too much for him. He asked if he might put forward my name to Her Majesty as his successor."

"So that was . . . why he . . . came!" Zenobia murmured.

"That was why, and although I have known Cecelia for some years, I had no more intention of marrying her than of marrying anybody else."

His lips moved against her cheek before he went on:

"Except the perfect woman whom I was looking for to take the place of my mother, who occupied a secret shrine in my heart which I have never spoken of to anyone."

"Is that . . . really where I am . . . now?"

"You fill it completely!"

The Earl pulled her closer to him as he added:

"Because I know now why you hate society, and why, if

148

you are honest, you are a little afraid of what your life will be like with me."

Zenobia made a little murmur but the Earl went on:

"Let me re-assure you by saying that most of our time will be spent here at the Castle."

"Can we . . . really do . . . that?" Zenobia asked with a rapt note in her voice that he did not miss.

"It is what I have every intention of doing," he answered, "not only because I love and adore you, my precious. I have no wish for you to be spoilt by the admiration you will receive in London, which will make me very jealous, but also for two other reasons."

"What are . . . they?"

"First, as Lord Lieutenant I shall have a great many duties in the County, and secondly, I had a visitor to luncheon who wants me to collaborate with him in building a new race-course in this part of England."

"You mean Lord Ventnor?" Zenobia said.

"You knew that was who came to luncheon with me?" the Earl asked. "He is not only a very attractive man in himself, but also an inveterate gossip. So I did not wish him to see you."

"You are so . . . sensible," Zenobia sighed, "and I am very . . . foolish."

"You were foolish not to trust me, and very, very foolish not to be aware, as we are so close to each other, that I loved you."

"I . . . I did not think it . . . possible, not after all I had . . . heard."

"Of the women in my life?" the Earl enquired. "Of course, but they were never of any real importance to me, and none of them, even if it had been possible for me to marry them, could have qualified for my secret shrine, which was empty until you filled it."

He did not wait for Zenobia to answer, but kissed her until she was breathless.

Then he said:

"Now all the explanations have been made, and all we have to do, my darling, is to wait, which will be intolerable, until after the Funeral, when I can make you mine."

"Nothing matters...as long as I become...your wife," Zenobia said. "I will hide in the cellars, or in the dungeon, if you have one. Then when we are married I will do...everything in my power to make you...happy and keep you...loving me."

The Earl knew it was a vow, and he said quietly:

"That is what I want, and I am betting on a certainty when I know we will be blissfully happy together."

Then he was kissing her again.

At last, thinking of him rather than of herself, Zenobia said:

"You must go to bed! You have had a long day, and I cannot understand why you did not go upstairs as soon as the Lord Lieutenant left."

"That is what I meant to do," the Earl said, "but I sat thinking of you, and time seemed to slip by until, thank God, I was there when you needed me."

"It was fate that I should...find you when I was so...frightened."

"A fate that has been very kind to us," the Earl replied. "And now, my darling, I will go to bed if you want me to, because I think you, too, must rest and forget everything, except that I love you!"

He drew her to her feet.

They walked from the Silver Salon hand-in-hand and up the stairs.

Only as they reached the landing did Zenobia say:

"You may think it very...banal that I should think such

things . . . but could I please have a . . . new gown in which to be . . . married? I came here with only the things I thought I should need, and which I wore in Devonshire when I was with Papa."

The Earl smiled.

"You shall have the most beautiful gown any bride has ever had," he said, "but even if it is made of moonlight and decorated with stars, it will not be beautiful enough for you!"

Outside her bedroom he kissed her.

Then as she went inside he said:

"You are not frightened? You do not mind being alone?"

"Now now," Zenobia said happily.

"Lock both your doors," he said, "and when you say your prayers, tell the angels to look after you until I can do so both by day and by night."

She lifted her lips to his.

He kissed her again before he went quietly towards his own room.

She shut her door and locked it as he had told her to do.

Then she crossed the room to lock the door into the Sitting-Room.

As she did so she was aware that the curtains were drawn back as she had left them and the window was open.

She looked at the beauty outside and felt her whole being rise in a paean of praise towards the sky.

"Thank You, God, Thank You!" she said.

There were no words in which to express her happiness.

*　　*　　*

The next morning Lucy came in answer to her bell.

She exclaimed in surprise when she saw the packed trunk in the centre of the room.

"Why ever did you trouble to do that yourself, Miss?"

she asked. "I only got 'Is Lordship's order about fifteen minutes ago!"

"What order?" Zenobia enquired.

"'Is Lordship sent a message to say that as there'd be so many relatives staying for Her Ladyship's Funeral, you was to move up to the Nurseries on th' Second Floor."

Lucy spoke as if she were remembering what she had been told.

Then she said hastily:

"I don't suppose you know, Miss, that Lady Mary died last night. Doctor's been an' says it were heart failure."

"I am very sorry to hear that," Zenobia replied. "I hope she did not suffer."

"Oh, no, Miss. The Doctor says as 'ow he thought she'd a pain in her chest and lay down on her bed—fully dressed she was—and knew no more."

She added, pleased to be informative:

"The Funeral's to be on Saturday. It seems a bit of an 'urry, but there—it's gloomy in a 'ouse where someone's dead!"

"That is true," Zenobia said, remembering how miserable it had been when her father died.

She could not help feeling it was pathetic that nobody should mourn Lady Mary.

From what Lucy said, as she chattered away helping her dress, the staff were delighted.

Now they would no longer be found fault with.

She was certain, too, that Mr. Hedges was sighing with relief.

Lady Mary could no longer be disagreeable about the books in the Library.

She said very little, except to inform Lucy what she knew had been relayed downstairs—that her work for the Exhibition was very important.

"I must not waste time," she said, "not even for a Funeral, so I had better stay up here and get on with all I have to do."

"If you asks me, Miss," Lucy said, "'Is Lordship won't keep 'is relatives 'ere any longer than 'e can help. Most of them is old, and Mr. Bateson says are always beggin' 'Is Lordhsip to get married, and it annoys 'im."

Zenobia smiled to herself.

When she went upstairs she found the Nurseries filled with sunshine and very comfortable.

They also made her think of the Earl when he was a little boy.

There was his rocking-horse on which he must first have developed his love of horses.

There was his Fort which had fuelled his desire to be a soldier.

Also a book-case filled with the same children's stories that she had loved when she was little.

There was a large safety-guard in front of the fire and a low chair on which she thought his Nanny must have sat and nursed him.

On the walls there were pictures of angels, fairies, and goblins besides a very beautiful portrait of his mother, whom he had loved.

Zenobia had the feeling that the Nurseries welcomed her.

She knew it was not only because they were redolent of the years the Earl had spent there.

It was, too, because she prayed that one day her son would be in there.

He would ride the rocking-horse, play with the Fort, and sleep in the prettily decorated night-nursery.

The first night before the Earl's relatives arrived, she

thought it was impossible to be any happier than she was at the moment.

She had dined downstairs with the Earl.

She knew that they were both savouring every moment they could be together.

When his guests crammed into the house, they would be separated.

"If they had one glimpse of you, darling," the Earl said, "they will know that I am head-over-heels in love. When we finally marry, and God knows it will seem like several centuries before it is Saturday, I have no wish for them to have any memories of 'Miss Webb.'"

"I thought you found her rather...useful!" Zenobia teased.

"I find her adorable, irresistible, and far too lovely to be seen by anybody but me!" the Earl said firmly.

He pulled her roughly into his arms as he added:

"Why could we not be Bedouins or Turks so that you would have to cover your face and no man could see you except your husband?"

Zenobia laughed.

"Is that what you want me to do?"

"Of course I want it!" he said. "At the same time, being English, I want you to help me in everything I do, in everything I think."

He saw the light in Zenobia's eyes and added:

"You will have to assist me to design the race-course, you will have to take up your duties as a Lord Lieutenant's wife, and, of course, more important than anything else, you will have to look after me."

His voice deepened as he went on:

"You must heal me if I am sick and, please God, fill the Nurseries, where you are sleeping now, with our children."

As it was just what she had thought herself, Zenobia blushed.

"I know you have been thinking the same thing," he said, "and, darling, nothing could be more exciting or more wonderful than to see you holding my son in your arms."

"Supposing . . . it is a . . . girl?" Zenobia asked.

"In that case," the Earl smiled, "we shall have to try again!"

It flashed through both their minds that Lady Mary had been the first child.

It had been disastrous for her that she was a girl.

Almost as if he had spoken aloud, Zenobia said:

"I feel our . . . prayers will give . . . us as our first child . . . a son."

The Earl kissed her and she knew she had excited him.

She felt the fire on his lips and saw the flicker of flames in his eyes.

Then he left her.

She knew that from early the next morning, he would be out of reach.

Zenobia sat down at the table in the Nursery and wrote all the letters that were still outstanding.

When she had finished, she sent a footman to Mr. Hedges.

She asked him if there were any other books that she should read which might describe other treasures that were available.

When the books were brought to her, she forced herself to read them.

It was very difficult to think of anything but the Earl and wish she was beside him.

When Friday morning came, there was no sign of her wedding-gown.

She began to be afraid that the Earl has forgotten when there were so many other things for him to think about.

It was not that she really minded.

When she married him it would be wonderful.

In fact, so perfect for both of them that her clothes were of secondary importance.

Yet she was woman enough to want to look beautiful on the most important day of her life for the man she loved.

She thought she might send him a note to remind him.

Then she told herself it would be a very banal thing to do.

She had had a note from him every morning and evening.

They came upstairs concealed among other papers that were quite unimportant.

But the footmen who carried them would not suspect he was communicating with her except as concerning their work together on the Exhibition.

When the first note arrived she had turned over the papers rather listlessly.

She wondered why he thought them worth sending up to her, then when she found the note, her whole being seemed to come alive.

It was short, but very loving.

Later in the evening she was thinking of him wistfully.

Another note, again concealed among some papers, arrived.

She sat down to read it and found it was two pages long.

It told her how much he loved her, how every minute they were apart was intolerable.

I longed to come upstairs to tell you of my love, my precious and beautiful wife-to-be, but because I am protecting you, as I will always do, I know it would be a mistake.

Servants talk and invariably notice everything that is unusual. My grandmother and a number of my aunts have brought their lady's-maids with them, who, I am quite certain, are inveterate gossips.

I am therefore controlling myself in a manner which I find extremely boring, but which I know is right.

I love you and adore you, and all my life is dedicated to you from now until eternity...

Zenobia kissed the letter and slept with it under her pillow.

On Saturday morning another letter arrived.

With it were a number of dress-boxes that had been sent from London by train.

She waited until she was alone before she unpacked them.

When she did so, she found that one contained the most beautiful wedding-gown she had ever imagined.

Because it was so beautiful and so exquisitely made, she knew the Earl must have had a great deal of experience in the past.

It did not make her jealous.

This time he was choosing a wedding-gown for someone he really loved.

That made it unique.

The hours of Saturday seemed to pass like centuries.

She kept looking at the clock to see if it had stopped.

She was aware that the Funeral cortège had left the house early.

It had made its way to the village Church that was just inside the Park gates.

It was Lucy who had told her that Lady Mary's coffin was carried on a farm-wagon.

It was covered completely with flowers and drawn by two horses.

Six pall-bearers walked on either side of it.

Behind them came the Earl on foot followed by the carriages containing the relations.

"It were very impressive, Miss, t'were really!" Lucy related. "We all had t'attend th' Service in th' Chruch which were very beautiful, but only th' family followed the coffin to th' vault, and 'Is Lordship were t'only one as went inside."

Lucy paused for breath.

Then she said:

"No one was cryin' an' it seemed strange at a Funeral. but there, 'Er Ladyship were sharp wi' everyone, not only us servants. I've 'eard 'er ever so rude to 'er relations when they comes 'ere."

"I think now, Lucy, we should forget that," Zenobia said, "and try only to remember the nice things about her."

Lucy walked towards the door.

"There weren't none!" she said, determined to have the last word.

Zenobia was not listening.

She felt as if with Lady Mary's Funeral one chapter of her life had ended.

Now another was beginning.

It seemed to glow with all the radiance of a rainbow.

She would be with the Earl.

She knew it would be impossible for any two people to be happier than they were.

She had, however, still some time to wait before she could see him.

Lucy described the enormous luncheon that was taking place downstairs after the Funeral.

All the dignitaries in the County had come.

Not because they mourned Lady Mary, but because they wished to pay their respects to the Earl.

Lucy reeled off some of their names.

Zenobia was thinking of the next time there was a party at the Castle.

It would be when the Earl introduced her as his wife.

She vowed that in the future she would make sure that he was loved and respected by his neighbours as his father had been.

The tales of his love-affairs in London and the women who broke their hearts over him would be forgotten.

At long last it was time for her to dress.

The Earl sent her a message that she was to come downstairs at seven o'clock.

With the message came a box containing a lace veil which had been in his family for generations.

There was also a tiara made entirely of diamond stars.

Zenobia knew that the Earl had chosen this.

He was thinking of the night when they had looked at the stars together and he had kissed her.

She had felt then as if he carried her up to them.

Their brilliance was burning in them both.

In the letter that had come in the morning he had given her permission to tell Lucy what was intended.

But she was to swear her to secrecy.

He wrote:

I expect eventually all the servants will know what is
happening, but just for to-night, I would like to keep
it between Williamson, Bateson, my valet, and your
maid.

Lucy was thrilled at being told Zenobia was to marry
the Earl.

"I'm not surprised, Miss!" she said when Zenobia told
her. "You're the prettiest lady I've ever seen in my life, an'
certainly the prettiest that's ever come 'ere!"

She gave a rapturous sigh before she added:

"'Is Lordship's that 'andsome that no other gentleman
could ever touch him, so the two of you together makes me
think you must 'ave stepped out of a fairy-story."

"That is exactly what it is," Zenobia said, "and that is
why, Lucy, we want to keep it a secret from everyone else
in the Castle."

She was very serious as she went on:

"You must promise me on everything which is sacred
not to tell anybody we are being married until it can be
announced publicly."

"I promise, of cors' I promise," Lucy cried. "Oh, Miss,
it's so exciting, an' ever so romantic!"

Zenobia laughed.

It was what she felt herself.

Lucy had dressed her in the beautiful gown which had
come from London and arranged the lace veil over her hair.

She set the diamond tiara on top of it.

Zenobia hoped that the Earl would think that she graced
his sacred shrine.

She knew he filled her heart and there was no man in
the world except him.

So she prayed that she would always fill his.

Mr. Williamson came to the Nurseries.

He told her he was to escort her down a side staircase.

This was so that she would not be seen by the footmen on duty in the hall.

The staircase led directly to the wing where the Chapel was situated.

When, after what seemed a long walk, they drew nearer to it, Zenobia could hear the soft music of an organ.

There were white flowers on the altar and big bowls of white lilac filled the Chancel.

The light from the candles revealed the exquisite eighteenth-century stained-glass windows and the ancient carved pews.

But Zenobia had eyes only for the Earl.

He was waiting for her at the door of the Chapel.

She thought as she looked at him that she could never have imagined a man's eyes could speak so clearly of love.

She put her hand on his arm.

He led her up the aisle to where his Chaplain was waiting for them.

Apart from Mr. Williamson and Bateson, who was the second witness, there was nobody else in the Chapel.

Yet to Zenobia it was filled with the music of the spheres.

She felt her father was there. She was sure that the Earl's mother was beside him.

The Chaplain read the beautiful Service with a deep sincerity.

When the Earl placed the ring on Zenobia's finger, she felt as if the angels were singing.

As they received the Blessing they were both enveloped with a light.

It came not only from God but from within themselves.

Then, as she moved from the Chapel on the Earl's arm, he took her up the side-staircase.

He opened the door of the Master Bedroom and they went inside.

He shut the door.

Taking her in his arms, he said:

"Now, at last, my precious, you are my wife, and I can tell you how much I love you!"

He kissed her very gently.

She knew that the solemnity of their marriage made them feel as if they were still part of the spiritual world.

The Earl took the wreath of stars from Zenobia's head.

He lifted off her veil and kissed her again before he said:

"Now we are going to eat our first meal together as man and wife. I cannot tell you, my darling, how much I have missed you these last three days!"

"And I you," Zenobia murmured.

"How I have looked forward," the Earl went on again, "to listening to the enthralling and exciting way your brain works differently from anybody else's!"

Zenobia laughed.

It was something she had not expected him to say.

He led her through the communicating-door to his Sitting-Room.

It was decorated with lilacs, carnations, and roses.

It looked very different from the austerity and masculinity which she had noticed when she had first found him there.

There was a table laid for dinner in the centre of the room.

The only light came from a huge gold candelabra. It held six candles, and white orchids surrounded it.

A garland went from one end of the mantelpiece to the other.

Other garlands draped the pictures by Stubbs and spoke of love rather than horses.

The Earl smiled at the excitment on Zenobia's face as she looked round.

"Williamson is responsible for all this," he said, "and it is something which he and Bateson contrived together and kept a close secret from everybody in the house. So you must thank them not me."

"It is lovely!" Zenobia exclaimed.

"That is what I think," the Earl replied.

He was looking at his wife as he spoke.

As everything was so secret, only Bateson and the Earl's valet waited on them.

The dishes were delicious.

But Zenobia could only think that she was eating and drinking the food of the gods.

When the meal was over, they sat talking together.

There was so much to say because they had been apart for the last few days.

So much for Zenobia to tell the Earl which she had kept secret until now.

"There must be no secrets between us in the future," he said, "and if you try to deceive me again, my darling, by pretending to be a secretary with the very mundane name of 'Webb,' I shall punish you—but with kisses!"

"I . . . I would like . . . that," Zenobia replied softly.

The Earl rose to his feet.

"To-night," he said, "because only a few people know what is happening, we are sleeping in my room. But when we return to the Castle after our honeymoon you shall use the rooms that were my mother's. I feel, my darling, she would like you to be in them."

Zenobia was very touched by what he said.

She went into his bedroom.

She found that everything was laid out for her on the great velvet-curtained four-poster bed.

It was where generations of Ockendons had slept.

The candles were lit, and, as she half-expected, the curtains were drawn back so that they could see the stars.

There was no valet and no lady's-maid, and the Earl said:

"I wanted to be alone with you, my darling, and God knows, I have waited long enough!"

"I . . . I wanted to be . . . with you."

He pulled her gently to him, but for a moment he did not kiss her.

He only looked down at her face.

Her eyes were shining as she looked up at him, her lips parted.

He knew that her heart was thumping in her breast and echoing his.

"How can you be so beautiful, so perfect?" he asked. "How can you be everything I have always wanted as my wife, and was quite certain I would only find in Heaven?"

"That is . . . where I feel I am . . . now," Zenobia whispered.

Then his lips were on hers, possessive and demanding.

She knew he asked the complete surrender of herself as he held her closer and closer.

She knew that just as they felt the same, so they thought the same and were indivisible.

He kissed her until the stars seemed to come through the windows to encircle them.

He undid her wedding-gown.

As it fell to the floor, he lifted her up in his arms and laid her down gently in the great bed.

For a moment she was hardly aware what he was doing.

She was bemused by his kisses, bewildered by sensations she had never known before.

They were not only Divine but also very human.

"I . . . love you . . . I love you," she tried to say.

Then he was beside her.

She could feel the strength and hardness of his body.

She wanted, although she did not quite understand, to melt into it so that she literally became a part of him.

She was not certain whether they spoke to each other and said aloud what they were feeling.

All she knew was that as the Earl kissed her, touched her, and made her his, a light seemed to blaze down upon them from the stars.

It brought healing and beauty as it entered their hearts.

It was also an ecstasy and rapture that was inexplicable in words.

It was in itself the language of the gods.

"You are mine, my darling, my lovely one, my wife!" the Earl said.

She may have heard it only in her heart.

"I am yours . . . completely and absolutely yours . . . now until the end of the world!" she whispered.

Then the light became blinding.

The stars were in their eyes and their hearts.

They were together in a secret shrine.

It was filled with love—the love which comes from eternity and goes on into eternity.

It is the creation of God—it is Life.

Barbara Cartland, the world's most famous romantic novelist, who is also an historian, playwright, lecturer, political speaker and television personality, has now written over 450 books and sold over 450 million books the world over.

She has also had many historical works published and has written four autobiographies as well as the biographies of her mother and that of her brother, Ronald Cartland, who was the first Member of Parliament to be killed in the last war. This book has a preface by Sir Winston Churchill and has just been republished with an introduction by Sir Arthur Bryant.

Love at the Helm, a novel written with the help and inspiration of the late Admiral of the Fleet, the Earl Mountbatten of Burma, is being sold for the Mountbatten Memorial Trust.

Miss Cartland in 1978 sang an Album of Love Songs with the Royal Philharmonic Orchestra.

In 1976 by writing twenty-one books, she broke the world record and has continued for the following nine years with twenty-four, twenty, twenty-three, twenty-four, twenty-four, twenty-five, twenty-three, twenty-six, and twenty-two. She is in the *Guinness Book of Records,* as the best-selling author in the world.

She is unique in that she was one and two in

the Dalton List of Best Sellers, and one week had four books in the top twenty.

In private life Barbara Cartland, who is a Dame of the Order of St. John of Jerusalem, Chairman of the St. John Council in Hertfordshire and Deputy President of the St. John Ambulance Brigade, has also fought for better conditions and salaries for Midwives and Nurses.

Barbara Cartland is deeply interested in Vitamin Therapy and is President of the British National Association for Health. Her book *The Magic of Honey*, has sold throughout the world and is translated into many languages. Her designs "Decorating with Love" are being sold all over the U.S.A., and the National Home Fashions League named her in 1981, "Woman of Achievement."

In 1984 she received at Kennedy Airport America's Bishop Wright Air Industry Award for her contribution to the development of aviation; in 1931 she and two R.A.F. Officers thought of, and carried, the first aeroplane-towed glider air-mail.

Barbara Cartland's Romances, (a book of cartoons) has been published in Great Britain and the U.S.A., as well as a cookery book, *The Romance of Food*, and *Getting Older, Growing Younger*. She has recently written a children's pop-up picture book, entitled *Princess to the Rescue*.